MW01135105

Enchant: Beauty and the Beast Retold

DEMELZA CARLTON

Book 1 in the Romance a Medieval Fairy Tale series

This is a work of fiction. Names, characters, businesses, places, events and incidents are either the products of the author's imagination or used in a fictitious manner. Any resemblance to actual persons, living or dead, or actual events is purely coincidental.

Copyright © 2017 Demelza Carlton

Lost Plot Press

All rights reserved.

ISBN-13: 978-1541399457

ISBN-10: 1541399455

DEDICATION

This one's for all the lovely ladies at the Women's
Business School.
Sometimes those crazy ideas pay off, I promise.
It might just take a little magic…

One

Three girls perched on the battlements, breaking their fast in the watery spring sun as they discussed the lone rider they'd spotted from their tower room.

"I think he's a knight come to sue for my hand in marriage," declared Anita, the oldest.

Arya sniffed. "Your hand isn't the bit he's most interested in, I'm sure. Anyway, knights wear armour, and he has none. I think he's one of Father's sea-captains, come to tell good news about his voyage."

Anita nudged Zuleika, the youngest, with her slipper-clad foot. "What say you, baby sister? Is he a knight or a sailor?"

Zuleika closed her eyes and cast her mind toward the man. She alone of the three had inherited her mother's skill for magic, and she practiced whenever she was able. "He comes with grim purpose. A duty he fears but will perform. I can't help but feel he carries my fate."

"Father wouldn't promise you in marriage to anyone until he's found husbands for the two of us. You're safe," Arya said. "Anita had better take a closer look, to make sure he's handsome enough for her."

Anita hushed them both as the man reined in his horse before the closed gate.

"Open up in the name of the king!" the man in the king's colours demanded, rapping smartly on the gate with his gloved fist. "I ride at the king's command and woe betide those who stand in my way!"

Safe behind the crenellations, Zuleika called, "What is the king's command?" She stuck her head out so she could see the man's face, though her sisters tried to pull her back.

"I bring a summons for the Lady Zoraida. The king has need of her." The man brandished a scroll case.

Zuleika's heart sank. This was a matter of magic, she was certain of it. The king would not be happy when he found out her mother had died two winters past of an ailment that stole her breath until she breathed her last. Even her mother's healing powers had been no match for it. "Then you'd better come in. I'll order the guards to open the gates."

Her sisters hissed at her to stop, for Father had ordered the gates kept closed for their protection until his return.

"He's one man," Zuleika said. "But if we don't let him in, he will return with an army to bring down the walls. I will do as he asks, and send him on his way. Father need never know."

This last was a lie, she knew, but it worked to calm her sisters. Zuleika's heart pounded in her chest, for today she would step into her mother's shoes and become the enchantress.

Two

Zuleika ordered the steward to serve the man refreshments in the dining hall while her maids dressed her hair. Like her sisters, she often wore hers uncovered, but if this strange messenger wanted to consult with the lady of the house, then she would dress like one.

She had learned at a young age how to step silently through the rushes that covered the stone floors. So when she appeared at the man's side, almost from nowhere, she had the satisfaction of seeing him start.

He recovered quickly, and bowed. "Lady Zoraida. I am Sir Ryder, a messenger sent from the king. I am to give you this and await your reply." He held out the scroll case gingerly, as though he thought it might bite him.

Zuleika resisted the urge to transform the case into something with teeth, and took it from him instead.

She unrolled the scroll, and read the message twice before she dropped it on the table next to Sir Ryder's empty ale cup.

"Do you know what this says?" she demanded.

He dropped his gaze to the rushes, crackling under this shuffling feet. "Mostly, my lady. If you don't accompany me back to the capital, I'm to take your children instead."

Only a coward threatened children. "Then King Thorn shall have his curse," Zuleika vowed. "But it comes at a price. He must leave my family alone."

"You have my word, Lady Zoraida."

Zuleika waved to summon a servant. "Prepare a room for Sir Ryder. I'm sure he wants rest after his long journey. I shall be in my bower." Her mother's bower, but the knight didn't need to know that.

"Yes, my lady." Mildred looked worried enough not to expose Zuleika's subterfuge. "If you will follow me, sir?"

Zuleika held her head high as she marched out of the hall and toward the stairs that led to the tower that had been her mother's. It was no different to the maidens' tower she shared with her sisters, and yet...it was a completely different world. Mother's bower held her books and scrolls; all her favourite curios from her travels all over the world, and seemed filled with the heady power of potential, of what might be.

When Zuleika crossed the threshold today, destiny wrapped around her. The room might be filled with her mother's things, but it was her domain now.

Three

Zuleika rode alongside Sir Ryder, her head filled with as much doubt as her belly felt full of butterflies. Not about the curse she had created at the king's command. She knew her spell was perfect. Perhaps she had been a little heavy-handed on the curse aspect, but it was her first and she intended it to be a powerful one. No, her fears were far simpler. She had never travelled outside her father's lands before and to go to the capital for an audience with the king terrified her more than she was willing to admit. This was destiny at work, she knew, but that didn't mean she had to like it.

The journey seemed almost too short, for in no time at all she found herself riding through the gates at

Sir Ryder's side. Their arrival at the palace provoked a flurry of activity. A small army of maids flanked her and hustled her into a sumptuous apartment, where they washed the dust from her skin, dressed her hair in a fashionable style, and laced her into a gown fit for court.

The lavender gown suited her, for it was only a shade lighter than her violet eyes. The maids had pinned her long hair to the back of her head and so weighty was it that she found it a challenge to bow her head even the slightest bit. Instead, she was forced to lift her nose into the air like the most prideful princess imaginable. How her sisters would laugh if they could see her now.

When Sir Ryder returned to escort her to the throne room, Zuleika expected to see the whole court present. However, she found the room empty except for herself, Sir Ryder and the stern-looking man seated on the throne – the king, she presumed. She dropped a brief curtsey, as her mother had taught her, before raising her gaze to meet the king's.

His eyes hardened. "You are not Lady Zoraida," the king said. He turned to Sir Ryder. "I ordered you to bring me a witch, not some little girl."

Sir Ryder started to stammer out an excuse, but Zuleika was having none of this.

"You sent a letter demanding a curse, or her

children," Zuleika said. "So that my mother may lie peacefully in her grave, I came in her stead, carrying the curse you desire so ardently. And I am no child, but a woman grown." This last was stretching the truth a little, but Zuleika knew girls were often wed at younger than her sixteen years. Besides, she knew no child could create the powerful curse she carried for the king.

The king waved imperiously. "So, cast your curse then, girl, for your insolence tries my patience."

Zuleika's eyes flashed. "I already have."

"Your Majesty," Sir Ryder corrected. "His Majesty King Thorn prefers to be addressed as 'your Majesty'."

Zuleika saw more arrogance than majesty in King Thorn's demeanour, but she chose not to argue. "Your Majesty," she said. "I have created the curse you require, and cast it on this looking glass. It is no ordinary looking glass, but one which allows the beholder to see any person or place they desire, no matter how distant." She unwrapped the bundle in her hands and held up her mother's looking glass. "The moment your enemy looks into the mirror, he is cursed."

The King gestured for a servant to bring the mirror to him. His large hands dwarfed the delicate item. "Anyone who looks in this mirror is cursed or just my enemy?"

"The owner of the looking glass is cursed by gazing into it," Zuleika said. "Your Majesty," she added as an afterthought.

King Thorn's brow creased. "So if I send my enemy this farseeing mirror as a gift, the first time he uses it, he will be cursed, correct?"

Zuleika nodded.

"But if I were to look into it now," the king said, "will the curse harm me?"

Once again, Zuleika nodded.

King Thorn passed the mirror to a servant, who wrapped it carefully back in its cloth. "When my enemy gazes into his gift, what will happen?"

Zuleika swallowed. "His reflection will reveal the darkest, most beastly aspects of his nature, which will become visible to all those who look at him. His lands will no longer offer welcome; they will appear forbidding to anyone who approaches them. His castle walls will appear impossibly high. The entrance to his lands will disappear, along with all those who are loyal to him. He will be hideous, friendless and doomed to live in the dreariest place in the world, because he carries his curse with him wherever he goes." Zuleika couldn't help but express her pride in what she felt was a curse worse than death.

The king laughed. "So he will have no army, no supporters, and no woman would look at him for long enough to bear his sons." He clapped his hands. "You have done well, little witch. I think I shall keep you." He dismissed her with a wave of his hand.

"But my family, your Majesty," protested Zuleika. "Your letter said if I cast this curse, then my family would be safe."

King Thorn rose to his feet, no longer smiling. "You dare question the king's honour, girl? I gave my word that your family will be safe, and so they shall be. You, however, seem to lack the most basic womanly virtues of silence and obedience. In my service, you will learn both." He beckoned to Sir Ryder. "Take her to her room, and see that she stays there."

Four

Zuleika ate little at dinner, retiring early. She worried what her father would think when he returned home to find her missing. Did the king intend to keep her prisoner forever? Not that her sumptuous chamber was anything like a prison cell. She knew there were dungeons beneath the palace where the king kept and tortured his prisoners. Enchantress or not, she was not powerful enough yet to avoid the cells if she displeased the king.

Despite the crackling fire, she shivered in her thin shift and crept into bed. Beneath the blankets, she could believe she was safe at home in the tower room she shared with her sisters.

At least, she could until the door creaked open and the king walked in. He wore none of the finery he'd sported in the throne room earlier that day. In fact, if it weren't for his short tunic, the man would be completely naked.

Zuleika sat bolt upright in bed, pulling the sheets up to her chin. "Your Majesty," she began uncertainly, "I believe you may have wandered into the wrong chamber." She swallowed. "You see, this one is mine."

"Everything in this kingdom is mine," the king said. "This palace. This chamber. Everyone and everything in it." He seized her blankets and ripped them from the bed. Cold seeped through the thin sheet that was now Zuleika's only covering, before he tore that away, too.

She scrambled out of bed. "Then I shall find somewhere else to sleep, sire," she said, trying to hide the tremor in her voice.

He strode forward so they stood face-to-face, though he towered over her. "Did you not hear me, girl?" He pointed at the bed. "Take off your shift, lie down and serve your king." As if to demonstrate, he pulled off his own tunic, so he stood in all his naked glory.

Zuleika did not find him glorious at all. Shaking with fury, she said, "You said my family would not be harmed. You lied. A king with no honour is no king at all."

King Thorn slapped her face so hard she landed on the bed, stunned. "Before you open your mouth again, you will remind yourself that silence and obedience are a woman's greatest virtues." With one mighty hand, he tore away her shift. "It is an honour to lie with the king and bear his children, even if they are bastards." He climbed onto the bed, pinning her beneath his weight.

Zuleika tasted blood from where she'd bitten the inside of her cheek at his slap. She summoned all the power within her as she said, "Shed a single drop of my blood, and you will never sire a living child."

The king seized her throat so tightly, she could scarcely breathe. "To curse the king's treason, girl. But you are no witch. You are powerless. And I shall prove it by putting a bastard in your belly tonight. You will practice silence and obedience or I shall choke the life from you." His grip tightened, cutting off her air. "Do you understand, girl?"

Zuleika nodded.

A moment later, when the king took her maidenhead, she was grateful for his chokehold, for she didn't have the breath to scream.

Five

The king snored, yet another thing Zuleika did not like about the man. She dressed as silently as she could, determined to leave before he woke. She had little else but her lavender court dress to cover her blood-slicked thighs, but blood was power to an enchantress. She would wash when she was safe. She tiptoed to the courtyard. No one stirred as she dipped her fingertips in her own blood to cast her mother's best and least known spell: a portal to take her away from here.

She traced a doorway in the air. Now, instead of castle walls, she saw snowy peaks. The mountains near her home.

Zuleika glanced back, considering whether to claim

her mother's mirror back, complete with the curse, but she did not. The mirror was tainted by the king's touch, much as she had been, and she had honour, even if he had none. He and his enemy could have their curse, in exchange for her family's safety. She would flee and never return.

She paused only to pack a few things from her mother's bower before Zuleika opened another portal, to a beach, this time. In the warm, salty water, she washed all traces of King Thorn from her body, before she healed her hurts. There would be no child. The king might not believe it yet, but he had activated the spell she cast on him when he shed her blood. His fate was sealed.

Zuleika pulled her enchantress' mantle closer about her. She accepted her fate, but hers would be far brighter. This she swore on her mother's grave before she left it behind, too.

Six

"Master, Sir Ryder has arrived." Greta dropped a clumsy curtsey.

Prince Vardan looked up from his dinner. "Whatever is my brother's favourite lackey doing here?"

"Bringing you birthday gifts from the king," the knight replied, ambling into the great hall as though he and not Vardan owned it. He selected a saffron bun and bit into it. "He sends his best wishes upon your coming of age."

Vardan watched Sir Ryder devour the cake like he'd never eaten one before, choosing not to comment on the man's lack of manners in taking food before it was offered. That one pastry invoked the laws of hospitality, where neither would betray the other while they remained under the same roof. He didn't relax until the knight had washed it down with a mug of ale.

Then Vardan said, "But my birthday is still a fortnight away."

Sir Ryder shrugged. "His Majesty wanted to be certain his gifts arrived in time. Would you like to see them?"

Vardan's brother did nothing out of affection, he knew. There was no love lost between the brothers, especially not since Thorn had claimed the throne. Vardan had asked for, and been granted, what his brother had called the dubious honour of becoming the new Trade Master of Beacon Isle when he came of age. Vardan had thanked his brother and hightailed it out of the capital on the first available ship. If he hadn't, he was certain that he would either find poison in his food or be accused of some plot to assassinate the king. Besides, Vardan was not cut out for court life. The politics of the palace were too petty for him. He wanted to be doing things, and managing the country's largest and busiest harbour would be a welcome relief. He'd take a sea captain over a courtier any day.

"Did he send me a wife?" Vardan asked, only partly in jest. One of the other reasons he'd left court was because his brother had planned to marry him to some barren widow twice his age so that he could get his hands on the islands that were her dowry. When Vardan took a wife, he intended to marry for love, or at least for affection. He wanted a woman who enchanted him, not one who reminded him of his mother.

Sir Ryder laughed. "No. I think he's still looking for one of those himself. But if you fancy a ride…" He gestured toward the open doors.

Vardan gazed into the bailey, and was surprised to meet the eyes of a horse. Nothing like the sturdy ponies that roamed wild on Beacon Isle, this creature had all the hauteur of an emperor. Black as the ocean at night, he seemed to have the same seething turbulence, as if the moment a man had the temerity to mount him, the horse would show him no mere man could command the sea.

"He's magnificent. A mount suitable for a prince, or even a king. I'm surprised my brother was willing to part with him." Vardan approached the animal, whose bridle was held by Marshall, the head groom.

"Only the best for the prince, he said," Sir Ryder told him. "He wanted me to make certain the stallion is to your liking. I am not to leave until I have seen you ride him."

Vardan eyed the horse critically. "Tell me, has my

brother employed a witch? One who has cursed the horse so that when I attempt to ride him, I shall be thrown off and killed?"

Sir Ryder's eyes grew wide with what Vardan thought was genuine astonishment. "Your Highness, no! The king would never wish to curse the horse ridden by his beloved brother."

Vardan believed the knight, but he still didn't trust his brother. "Very well. Saddle him, Marshall, and let Sir Ryder have the first ride."

Despite the knight's protestations, in the end, Sir Ryder mounted the horse and took a turn around the bailey. The stallion's steady gait was as smooth as the rolling waves. A thing of beauty.

Reassured, Vardan accepted the reins from Sir Ryder and sprang into the saddle. A short walk took them to the gate, where Vardan urged the horse into a gallop. The fields beside the road flew past as Vardan laughed for sheer joy. His brother had given him a magnificent birthday gift. Perhaps Thorn finally felt secure enough in his kingship that he no longer imagined his younger brother as a threat to the throne. Vardan hoped so, for he had no intention of usurping his brother's place. He intended to live out his life as the Trade Master of Beacon Isle, the place he loved most. Every time he walked into his grandmother's rose garden, it was as if the old queen were alive once more, and he was a boy filled with hope for a future that seemed so bright. And now when he rode out on his water horse, which he would call...Arion, he decided, he could almost fly to the harbour to greet the ships coming in to trade goods from all corners of the world.

When he returned to the bailey, breathless with laughter and the thrill of the ride, he thanked the knight profusely for bringing his brother's gift, and told him to convey his gratitude to the king.

"There is another gift, more valuable still," the knight replied. He held out a beribboned box, big enough to hold a book, maybe two.

Yet when Vardan took the box, it felt too light to be books of any kind. "What is it?" he asked, shaking it.

Sir Ryder seized the box, stopping him. "It is very fragile, Your Highness. You must be careful."

Feeling like a chastened child, Vardan opened the package with exaggerated caution. Inside the box was a cloth-wrapped bundle, and inside the cloth was..."A lady's looking glass?" Vardan exclaimed, lifting the offending item up to the light. Oh, it was pretty enough, with jewels cunningly set into the shape of a flower on the back, and a quick rub of the surface revealed his reflection, staring back at him, trying not to laugh at such a strange gift.

"An enchanted looking glass," Sir Ryder corrected. "Now you are so far from the capital, the king wished you to be able to still see the goings-on at court. You merely have to breathe on the mirror, speak the name of a person or place, and when the mist clears, you will see what you seek, as clearly as if you were there. You could see the king at court, or his bride on their wedding day, without ever leaving your island. You could even peek at the future queen when she's bathing, to see if she is comely enough for the king." He winked.

Vardan tried to hide his disgust as he wrapped the mirror and stowed it back in its box. As if he would use such a powerful object to peep at women to stimulate his own lustful desires. Perhaps chivalry really was dead in the rest of the country. Not here on Beacon Isle, though. "Perhaps later," Vardan said. "Please convey my thanks to the king for his gifts. How long will you be staying? I shall have the servants prepare a room for you."

Conscious of being a good host, he made sure his guest was settled and that his staff knew to pay the knight every courtesy before Vardan carried the box to his solar.

Much later that night, weary of listening to Sir Ryder's tales of the latest intrigues at court, Vardan retired to his bedchamber.

Try as he might, he could not sleep. Could a magical object truly let him see things far away? And if it could, why would his brother part with something so valuable?

Finally, he rose from his bed and padded to his solar, where the mirror lay in a patch of moonlight. The flower on the back seemed to glow purple, but he was sure it was either his imagination or a trick of the light.

What would he want to see? Vardan truly had no desire to spy on women in the privacy of their chambers. Nor did he want to see his brother lording it over everyone in court. The *Whale*, one of the ships due this week, had been delayed, though, and there were tales of pirates to the north. If there were pirates in his shipping lanes, Vardan wanted to know as much about them as possible, so he or his small navy could hunt them down. The Trade Master of Beacon Isle had no mercy for pirates.

He breathed on the glass. "Show me the *Whale*." The looking glass glowed purple, and Vardan gasped in shock.

Seven

Zuleika travelled the world. Like her mother before her, she journeyed from place to place, seeking out those children who showed a spark of magic. Nothing like as powerful as hers, of course, but enough to make them dangerous without the knowledge they needed to control their powers. On their name day, she would appear to give the child a blessing, which in truth was the gift of knowledge they would need in later life. Once they discovered their powers, the girls – for they were always girls – would have the necessary knowledge to make use of them. Some girls were destined to be healers, while others possessed the power to communicate with animals. One girl appeared to have the extraordinary ability to manipulate destiny – not just her own but that of other people, too. Some had the gift of illusion, or power over plants and other simple creatures, and one particularly gifted child had the power to manipulate air currents. She looked forward to finding out how these girls chose to use their powers. For good, she hoped, so that they would follow her example.

Zuleika prided herself on being a good witch, by which she meant she did no harm to those who did not already deserve it. After all, she did not wish to end up like the djinn. Djinn were powerful magic users like herself who had used their powers for their own personal gain, to the detriment of others. When they caused so much trouble that they came to the attention of the rulers of the day, they had been sentenced to enslavement. Not to a person, but to an item, and anyone who possessed that item also possessed mastery over the djinn.

Of course, djinn were clever, and quite capable of influencing their masters. Recently, the ruler of a desert city had requested her assistance to rid himself of a particularly pesky djinn who insisted on tampering with the city's only water source. She'd dealt with the djinn, all right, cramming his loincloth-clad behind back into his lamp before hiding the lamp in a cave so protected with enchantments no one would release him. But when she returned to the city to collect her payment for a job well done, she found that the problems with the water supply had worsened in her absence. The man who'd hired her blamed her for the faults in his ancient plumbing and threw her out of the city. Or he tried to, anyway. An enchantress as adept at portal-casting as Zuleika was couldn't be kept out of anywhere for long. She'd taken great satisfaction in turning the ungrateful bastard into a frog, before tossing him into his own water supply so he could investigate the pipework himself. She'd left him a loophole, so he could break the curse, if he didn't want to live out the rest of his life as a frog, but she hadn't made it easy for him. Such was the life of a good witch.

She had returned home on occasion, ostensibly to check her mother's books and notes when she was asked to enchant items with unusual properties. That pair of dancing shoes, for instance, which the girl had managed to lose at a party, so that the prince pursued her all over the country to return her precious shoes.

First Arya, then Anita had found suitable men they wanted to marry, so both now lived with their respective husbands and, the last she'd heard, children, too. That left her father alone in the keep, so she made it a point to visit him as often as she was able. She only stayed for a day or two before leaving again – she didn't want the king to get word of her presence. There was no telling what that dishonourable man might do, to her or her father.

This time, when she arrived in her mother's bower, she found her father waiting for her. He started from the couch, as though from a deep sleep. Evidently, he had been waiting for some time.

"Hello, Father," she said. "What is wrong?"

"Zuzu, you're here," her father said, rubbing at his eyes. "My ships. I have lost all my ships. Wrecked, sunk, boarded by pirates... Who knows? But they are lost. And without them, we have nothing but this keep. I need your help, Zuleika. If anyone can find my lost ships, even one of them, for that would save our fortunes, it is you. Will you help me?"

"Of course, Father," she said warmly. "Which ship did you hear from last?"

"The *Rosa*. Her cargo was to be your dowry, dear girl. Purple silk, vair and amethysts exactly the colour of your eyes, to make you gowns fit for a queen. The king has not taken a wife yet, and I had hoped to send you to court so that you might enchant him. But the *Rosa* has disappeared, along with all your finery. She left port on schedule, but she should have arrived in the harbour by now. I fear all is lost."

Biting back a protest that she'd rather die than dress up for the king, Zuleika merely nodded. "I will not fail you, Father. I will find your ships and their cargo. If pirates have taken them, they will rue the day they were ever born." And searching for them would take her far from King Thorn, she thought but did not say.

Father fell to his knees. "Thank you."

A father should not kneel before his children, least of all to her, Zuleika thought, as she helped her father to his feet. "Think nothing of it. I am a dutiful daughter, nothing more." And one who had no desire to be queen.

Though she had been home scarcely more than a few minutes, Zuleika prepared to cast another portal, not to a place, but to a ship's deck. She bit her lip, tasted her own blood, touched her finger to her tongue, and drew the doorway. When her blood touched the earth, the doorway glowed and opened. Zuleika stepped through.

Eight

Zuleika took in a deep breath, as she always did when arriving at a new place. Except that this time, there was no air to breathe, only water. Deep beneath the surface, Zuleika's lungs filled with seawater, and she began to drown. Her flailing legs kicked something hard – the ship, or the seabed? She wasn't certain. Desperately, she drew a doorway, then another, and a third. No light meant no portal, and no portal meant she would die. Zuleika bit her finger, watching the blood stream in the current, as she drew a fourth doorway. She thought she glimpsed light, before her eyes were forced to close. It might have been a portal, or it might have been heaven beckoning her home.

She wasn't sure which she welcomed most, but darkness dragged her down, and she knew no more.

Nine

When Zuleika regained consciousness, she couldn't feel her body. The one exception was her throat, which burned like she'd swallowed liquid fire. She coughed weakly, relieved to find her ears still worked.

"What is it?"

"Is it a bird?"

"No, I saw a flash, like lightning. That be no bird."

"It's a girl!"

"A corpse, more like. She's not moving."

"Her dress is soaked through. She'll freeze, laying out here in the snow like that. Feel her skin. Cold as ice, she is."

"See? A corpse, like I told you."

"She's no corpse, you old fool! She still draws breath. We better get her inside and warm before she perishes of cold."

"But the master…"

Zuleika heard what sounded like a slap.

"Shhh. You'll scare the maid to death."

Zuleika wanted to tell her rescuers that she feared little any more, but her voice died in her damaged throat. For when she opened her eyes, she saw no one at all. Nothing but a walled garden, shrouded in snow. Her eyes drifted shut, and the darkness embraced her once more.

Ten

"With respect, master, it won't be enough. One, perhaps two more ships, and the cellars will be full. Your storehouses were full months ago. If we don't find a way to shift this cargo off the island soon – "

A bolt of what appeared to be purple lightning arrowed down from the cloudless sky, followed by a sharp crack that echoed off the courtyard walls.

Vardan waved Rolf into silence. "What in heaven's name was that?" the prince asked.

"Hopefully not something in the cellar," Rolf said drily.

Vardan laughed. "I hope you're right, my friend." He clapped his steward on the back and hurried to the nearest window overlooking the rose garden. At least, the expanse of snow smothering his grandmother's garden.

"It's a girl!" Inga exclaimed.

Vardan stared. Sure enough, the housekeeper was right. Lying on the snow was a woman whose scarlet dress made it look like she lay in a pool of blood. Perhaps she did.

"Is she hurt?" Vardan demanded.

Sven, the gardener, muttered something unintelligible.

"I don't think so, master," Inga called up. "Cold, yes, frozen nigh to death in her wet things outside in this weather, but her eyes opened for a moment there, and she still draws breath. We must get her inside before she takes a chill, if she hasn't already."

Most men would have called for more servants, Vardan knew, but he wasn't most men, and he was curious. Just as lightning did not strike out of a clear sky, women dressed in scarlet did not suddenly appear in rose gardens. Vardan smelled magic at work, but he wasn't yet certain whether it was good or ill. After what had befallen him, he no longer had any love for magic or those who practiced it.

He took the steps two at a time until he reached the garden, then trudged through the snow to where he could look upon the strange woman's face.

What he'd taken for a dark veil was instead the girl's unbound hair, as rich and dark as the sable furs in his nearly full cellar. He wondered idly whether her hair was also as silky to the touch. His hand reached out almost of its own accord.

"She's quite the beauty, isn't she, master? Though she's mighty pale. Perhaps it's the cold. With a little colour in her cheeks, there wouldn't be a man in the kingdom who could ignore her when she walks by," Inga said, as if reading his thoughts.

"She would not walk," Vardan found himself saying. "She would ride. A horse fit for a queen."

Inga cleared her throat. "Before you go riding with her, master, we must get her warm. Inside. For that we need a strong man more than a horse who can carry the maid – "

"I'll do it," he said. The girl was surprisingly heavy in his arms, but he realised that most of the weight was her waterlogged, half frozen clothes. "Have a room prepared for her. In the meantime, I will take her to my bed – "

Inga made a disapproving sound. "The queen's bedchamber would be better, master."

Though his grandmother no longer lived, they would always think of her favourite rooms as the queen's chambers. "Yes. Of course, you are right. I shall take her there."

He carried the mysterious girl up the steps to the corridor his grandmother had claimed as her own. The windowless bedchamber was exactly as she had left it, right down to her shell combs on the table.

"Put her on the bed, master," Inga ordered, and the prince obeyed.

He regretted it instantly, as his arms felt strangely empty once he released the girl. "Surely you should turn down the bed first, so I can place her under the covers? I wouldn't want her to be cold." He reached for her again.

"Not in her wet things. I'll help her into some dry clothes before I put her to bed, master," Inga said. She waited a moment, before she added, "I will have to undress her. It would be unseemly for you to stay."

It took a moment for Inga's words to register. Unseemly. Undress. No, he did not watch women undress without their knowledge. Whoever this girl was, she deserved to be shown every courtesy. Vardan wasn't sure what had come over him, that he could forget such a thing. Thank heaven Inga had taken the liberty of reminding him.

"Thank you," he said fervently. "Treat her as an honoured guest. Send word when she wakes."

He hurried back to his solar, where he was glad to find Rolf no longer waiting to discuss cellars, storehouses and other such mundane matters.

There was a woman in the house who occupied all of his thoughts. Pale features, dark hair, who rode into his rose garden astride a bolt of purple lightning. If his grandmother could see the girl in her chambers now, and the distraction she drove her grandson to, the old queen would call him a fool.

A fool who could think only about how the girl was being undressed in those chambers right now...

For the first time in his life, Vardan's fingers itched for the magic mirror that would allow him to see all that happened in the queen's bedchamber, but he resisted the urge. He would see plenty of the girl, for unless she could summon another bolt of lightning to ride away from the island, she would be trapped here for some time. Just like everyone else.

Eleven

Zuleika drifted in and out of consciousness, aware of women's voices rising and falling around her, but too drowsy to understand their words. She had a body, and a bed, or so it seemed, but her time in the ocean and in the snow afterwards had sapped so much of her strength that there was little else she could do aside from lie in bed and sleep.

Not since the night the king violated her had she felt so weak. No man had taken advantage of her this time, though, she was certain. Years ago, in a longhouse where victorious warriors believed they had the right to lie with any woman of their choosing on the night of a glorious victory, she had performed a tricky little spell on herself, intending it to be more of a precaution than necessary protection.

Instead, Zuleika had woken to find a man writhing in agony on the pallet beside her, while lightning coursed over her skin. No man had tried to touch her since, so she wasn't sure if the spell would be quite so strong a second time, but the lightning flared into life when anyone approached her with harmful intent, warning them away. She hadn't felt the tingle of her lightning shield here.

"She has such soft hands. Highborn, no doubt," one woman said.

"You should have seen the dress she arrived in. Silk, it was, I'm sure, though the water ruined it. Some princess, perhaps," a second female voice remarked.

"How'd she get here, then? Princess or no, she managed to make her way from the sea, through at least three locked gates, and into the master's rose garden. It must be magic, I tell you. Perhaps she is cursed, too."

"Well, aren't you a bushel of sunshine, then? Maybe destiny sent her here to break curses, but she won't do none of that if you scare her." A snort. "I ask you, does she look cursed to you? Not a mark on her, and I undressed her and put her to bed myself. Blessed, more like. Maybe she's exactly what the master needs."

The master could not have her, Zuleika thought,

digging her teeth into her lip. A single drop of blood was all it took to recast that lightning spell. Her body might be weak, but the magic in her blood was as strong as ever.

"Aren't you taking her tray?" the second woman asked.

"No, I'll leave it a little longer. She might wake, and want a bite to eat. If I ever slept as long as she has, I'm sure I'd be famished."

"Has she said anything yet?"

"No, not a word. Not even in her sleep. She is a mysterious maiden, this one."

The voices faded as the women left, Zuleika presumed. Still, she waited until she could no longer hear them before she dared to open her eyes.

The room looked as richly decorated as any of the rooms at the palace, though the bed hangings and the tapestries had faded over time. Whoever lived here was not as rich as they once were, or perhaps they'd simply placed her in one of their less sumptuous guest apartments. The walls were not plain stone, but plastered, so she definitely knew she wasn't in the king's palace.

She sat up cautiously, relieved to find no light-headedness. She didn't have time to be ill; she needed to find her father's ships. But for that, she would need her strength.

Zuleika examined the tray on the table beside her bed. A small loaf of bread, some fish and a jug of what she discovered with a cautious sniff was wine, not ale. Either she had travelled further south than she'd realised, or she was a guest in a prosperous house indeed. So whose was it?

Adding it to the long list of questions already burning in her mind, Zuleika broke her fast. She drank sparingly of the wine, knowing she would need her wits about her in this strange house.

When she was sated, she ventured out of bed. Her first few steps were tentative, but when she realised that she had regained enough of her strength to walk, Zuleika's steps quickened as she explored her chamber. The fine shift she wore, while not hers, was serviceable enough to protect her modesty, but it was hardly appropriate to wear once she left the room.

A chest at the end of the bed held gowns, but when Zuleika lifted one up, she found they were made in a fashion she had never seen anyone wear before, except in some of the old books her mother had inherited from her mother. Old gowns, in a chamber with faded hangings. The former owner of both no longer lived, Zuleika surmised, so she would not object to her borrowing her clothes.

She dressed in the most practical gown she could find, one of dark green wool. When she tried to place the matching veil on her head, the weight alone made her head ache, so Zuleika resolved to go with her head uncovered. She combed and braided her hair, wishing she owned combs as fine as these, carved of some sort of shell that caught the light and warmed it with rainbows.

If she met the master of the house, she would ask him what they were made of and where they were from, so she could travel there and obtain her own, Zuleika promised herself. In the meantime, she intended to explore the house and find out a little more about how she'd come to end up here.

Her door opened smoothly. Evidently, she was a guest and not a prisoner. The corridor outside her room was open to the frosty air, so she was glad she'd chosen wool and not linen. Nevertheless, she returned to her room to pull a cloak out of the chest to wrap around herself against the cold. Properly attired, she ventured out once more.

She peered over the sill of the glassless window and found the view as cold as the air. A courtyard smothered in deep snow, walled in so she couldn't see anything but the sea of white. Perhaps they did intend to keep her prisoner, and they felt the walls would keep her in so that no locks were necessary. The were certainly high enough.

Zuleika strode briskly along the colonnade, headed

for the shelter of a darkened corridor at the end that she hoped led deeper into the house. Torches burned in the wall sconces, leaving streaks of soot along the white-plastered walls.

She bit her lip, tasting blood once more, and whispered a seeking spell for her father's ship. The spell sparked and died. Her father's ship was too far away for her spell to reach it. Frustrated, Zuleika tried again, thinking of the silk her father had promised her when the ship came in. Silk she had no need for, but no matter.

The spell ignited in the air before her, weaving like a firefly as it led her deeper into the house. Zuleika stumbled after it, paying no heed to her surroundings as she followed the light to her destination – the cavernous cellars of the building. These were nothing like the cellars in her father's house, or the dungeon cells she'd seen in other places. These stretched beneath the building, the vaulted ceilings turning the warehouse into a veritable cathedral of commerce, for it was piled with goods of all kinds. Chests and barrels, stacks of timber, stone jars and bundles of cloth, statues and…she lost track of all the things she saw in the warehouse.

Her spell hovered over a particular chest, balanced precariously on top of two barrels. It was closed, but not latched shut, so she lifted the lid. Zuleika gasped at the sight of silk, exactly as her father had described it. This was her father's cargo…but where was his ship?

Her hand darted out, almost of its own accord, to stroke the fabric, as soft as she'd imagined. This silk had never touched the sea – salt would have marred its sheen. The chest had been removed from the ship before it sank to the depths where she'd nearly drowned. How, then, had it arrived here?

One thing was certain: whoever owned this house had no right to the stolen goods in his cellar. His wealth was no more his than any of these things. The master they spoke of was a dastardly pirate, the scum of the earth and every merchant's enemy. Whatever curse lay on him, she was certain he deserved it, and more.

She found a pry bar and began to open the tuns stacked around the chest, all marked with her father's brand. They were filled with vair, the grey-blue squirrel pelts royal courts found so fashionable of late. Carefully tucked between the pelts of a particularly full tun was a small chest, the size of her mother's jewel casket. Zuleika opened it with shaking hands. The chest was full of amethysts, all the same shade of violet she had seen so many times in her reflection. Just as her father had described them.

Zuleika sank to the floor, overcome by a mix of fury and frustration. More than half the room contained her father's cargo. A fortune in imports, which he believed lost. If this remained here, he was ruined. But if she could return it to him, even without his ships, he could buy new ones. And where were the crews? Had they perished when pirates attacked, or had they been enslaved? She was no innocent, she'd seen slavery the world over. No man or woman was spared hard labour when taken prisoner in war. But a pirate who sold slaves? The master here was despicable indeed. Perhaps Zuleika would turn him into a form fitting his nature. A pig, perhaps. A bristled boar. Or a form that would teach him the error of his ways? Then she should transform him into a minnow, or a small crab. Or perhaps a squirrel, covered in grey and white vair.

That would be fitting.

Zuleika rose. She added a squirrel pelt to the jewel casket and closed the lid. She tucked the chest of amethysts under her arm, striding out of the room to find somewhere she could cast a portal home to her father. She would show him the casket as proof that she had found his missing cargo, before she returned to this house to seek vengeance on the worthless pirate who had stolen it.

She marched through the corridors, searching for a way out that she simply could not seem to find. The snowy courtyard taunted her, but she could not cast a portal there. Smaller spells could be cast in air alone, but something as substantial as a portal needed to be anchored in earth – soil or natural stone, not the flagstones beneath her feet. The snow in the courtyard was too deep for her to reach the earth. She needed to leave the house and venture outside.

She whispered a spell to guide her to a way out, and found herself in what must be the great hall of the house. This was grander than her father's, its white walls stretching up to an arched ceiling much like the cellar downstairs. She had never seen a building like it. She crossed the room and reached for the bar fastening the great doors.

"Stop, thief!" Someone seized her around the middle.

Another set of hands snatched the chest from her grip as she fought her captors – more than one, she decided, as someone tipped her hood over her face, blinding her. She struck out behind her, hoping to land a blow on her cowardly assailant, or one of them, at least, but instead she tripped over the hem of her cloak. Her head hit the door she'd failed to open, and the blow stole her senses.

Darkness won once more.

Twelve

"I thought I told you to inform me when she awoke," Vardan said, staring down at the girl. Now she lay on the stone floor instead of the snow, but her closed eyes and the swelling bruise beneath her hair taunted him for being a bad host who did not properly protect his guests.

Inga must have run from the other end of the house, for she was still breathing hard. "Nobody told me, master. This is the first I knew of it, and it looks like she's no longer awake, anyway."

This wasn't Inga's fault, Vardan told himself, but it was hard to contain his anger. The girl was hurt, for heaven's sake.

"Who did this?" Vardan demanded. "She's just a slip of a girl. No need to clout her over the head. Inga here could probably restrain her."

Rolf coughed out a laugh. "She's more than a mere girl. Threw me across the corridor, she did, before she tripped over her own cloak and hit her head. I'll wager this one's a witch. How else did she get here?"

Vardan wet his lips. "I don't know, but I mean to ask when she wakes. Again. What did you say to her to make her attack you, Rolf?"

"I called her a thief." Rolf twitched the corner of her cloak aside and revealed a small casket. "She was carrying this."

Vardan lifted up the box. "From the cargo of the *Rosa*," he noted, tracing the merchant's mark on the side. He lifted the lid. "She's quite a discerning thief, then. A fine squirrel pelt, and a veritable treasure trove of jewels. What are these purple stones called?"

"Amethysts, master," Inga said. "Just the right shade to match that fur, too. The girl has a fine eye for colour."

A magical thief with fine eyes, who could match Rolf in a fight. Against all his normal inclinations to imprison her for being a thief, instead he felt the unfamiliar desire to protect her.

Vardan badly needed to speak to this girl. She sounded like the most remarkable woman he'd ever met, and he didn't even know her name yet.

"I'll take her back to her room, and this time, I intend to be there when she wakes up," Vardan said, once more scooping the girl up in his arms. Ah, that felt better. She was much lighter than before, though more heavily dressed, so her clothes must have been soaked through when she arrived. How had she made it from the ocean to his rose garden?

He added that to the list of things he wanted to ask her. In the meantime, he carried the welcome weight in his arms to her bed. After all, it wasn't like she could leave the island. She was trapped there as much as he was, whether she slept in a dungeon or the queen's bedchamber.

He settled her in her bed and sat down to wait. Answers would come soon enough

Thirteen

Some sound must have startled her into alertness, for Zuleika didn't wake willingly. Her head ached more than ever, but she strained to hear the noise again.

There it was – a breath, blown out forcefully as if in impatience.

Keeping her eyes closed, she cast her mind toward the heavy breather. A man, as she suspected. He radiated a strange combination of boredom and curiosity. Curiosity for the future, while he endured the tedium now. A guard, she guessed.

She opened her eyes slowly, expecting to see a dungeon, or at the very least, to find herself thrown outside into the snow. Instead, she saw she'd been placed in a bed. Possibly the very same bed she had recently vacated. She couldn't be certain, for in the dark room it was hard to discern whether there were hangings at all, let alone whether they were faded or not. What worried her most was that her lightning shield had not triggered when someone had attacked her. Either the spell was ineffective, which she doubted, or her assailant had not intended to harm her. Yet both explanations were impossible. Zuleika snorted. Enchantresses achieved the impossible on a daily basis.

"You may feign sleep for as long as you like, my lady, but you and I both know you are awake," a male voice said. It came from a shadow in the corner – a hulking shadow, but a man-sized one.

Years had passed, but Zuleika still heard that voice in her darkest dreams. He was no guard.

Try as she might, she would never forget King Thorn, and her very bones quaked in the terror invoked by hearing that voice. But she was not defenceless today. "Threaten me with whatever you wish. I will never remove the curse." She took a deep breath before continuing coldly, "It is no less than you deserve."

She prayed that he would not hear the frightened fluttering of her heart. Damn the king for what he had done, and for the memory possessing the power to scare her still. Zuleika vowed that she would leave this encounter the victor today. If he took so much as a step toward her, she would turn him into a toad. He deserved all that, and more.

As if he could read her thoughts, the man she thought was the king laughed. "You do not even know my name, let alone what a man like me deserves, though I daresay you are right. You must have been listening to servants' gossip, for only they believe that the curse can be removed. Who can blame them? They suffer, too, but they live in hope that the curse one day will be lifted. Why else would my storehouses be so full?"

Zuleika saw red. "Your storehouses are full of stolen goods which do not belong to you. The true owners slide into poverty, while you grow ever richer. That makes you a thief, sir, and a pirate. Synonymous with pond scum." She wished she had had the temerity to tell the king that when they first met. How dare a man who owned so much power already steal from upstanding merchants like her father? A toad was too good for him. A maggot might be more fitting.

Yet again, the man laughed. Zuleika began to wonder if she was in the presence of the king at all, or simply some madman who sounded like him. "You call me scum and sir in the same breath. As for my being a thief... That is what my servants say about you. They say you were caught carrying out a casket of jewels. What say you to that, Lady Thief?"

She bridled. "My father's ship was carrying those jewels home to me. I merely took what is mine. I am no thief."

"And neither am I, despite the contents of my storehouses. They, too, are the result of my curse, but if you have listened to the servants gossiping, then I am sure you know more than I do about our affliction. Tell me, lady: how would you break the curse?"

Dread settled in her stomach of a different sort. It dawned on her that this man wasn't the king, and she had no idea what he was cursed with. Even for an enchantress of her skill and power, tampering with an unknown spell was dangerous. And yet...breaking curses was what she was best at, though it wasn't as satisfying as animal transformations.

"I know nothing of your particular curse," she said cautiously, "but perhaps if I knew more, I might know someone who can help." Only a dark witch cursed those who did not deserve it. If he was cursed unjustly, she was honour-bound to help him. She drew herself up, trying to sound as authoritative as a queen, though she sat in her shift in the bed and not on a throne dressed in royal robes. "But only if you are not a pirate, and you swear that you intend to do no harm. Who are you, sir?"

The hunched shadow in the corner became a tall pillar of darkness as the man rose to his feet. "Lady, I am Prince Vardan, Trade Master of Beacon Isle, and no pirate. While you are my guest here, no one shall harm you."

He was right about that last part, Zuleika thought, but did not say. She wished she could see his expression, so she could judge if he was lying. It was on the tip of her tongue to tell him to step into the light, but if he sounded like the cursed king, and bore a curse of his own, he probably had been blessed with good looks to match those of the king. She had no desire to see Thorn's face or any like it ever again.

"And you are?"

Zuleika's mind raced. Beacon Isle was part of King Thorn's territory; which meant Prince Vardan must be his brother. That explained the similarity. If he knew her true identity, he might return her to the king. Not while she drew breath, she vowed. She would rather die than become King Thorn's whore. She chose to feign ignorance. "I am sorry, your Highness?"

For the third time he laughed. "You honestly can't expect me to believe that your parents named you 'Sorry'. Beauty or Belle I would believe. Especially Belle, for your voice does have bell-like qualities, and your beauty is already the talk of the house. In fact, if you do not give me your name, I shall give you one.

Lady Belle, the mysterious maiden who appeared in the snow."

"Your Highness is too kind," she murmured. "I am certain there are many ladies here far more beautiful than I."

Vardan barked out a laugh. "None that I have seen this week. But, as you say, you know nothing of curses. Least of all the kind of curse that turns a man into this." He unshuttered his lantern and held it high, so that she might see his face.

Zuleika recoiled in horror. What she had taken for a man, was in fact something so hideous she could scarcely bear to look at him. She wasn't even sure what creature he'd been transformed into. Some sort of monstrous…feline? Canine? Bear? And were those…tusks, or horns?

He lowered the lantern before she could decide, hiding himself in the shadows once more. There was no laughter this time. "So you see, Lady Belle, that there will be no breaking of my curse. Do you still wish to know more?"

What had he done to deserve such a fate? The curse she had visited upon his brother for her brutal rape was mild in comparison to this. Perhaps Vardan was a pirate after all, and a worse man than the king. If he deserved this curse, he would not dupe her into removing it. In the unlikely event that he had been cursed unjustly…then she would help him. But she would take her time to determine the truth of the matter before she made her decision.

"I do, your Highness," she said with her eyes closed.

"Then on the morrow, you shall have a tour of Beacon Isle." And with that, he swept out of the room.

Fourteen

He should never have unshuttered the lantern, Vardan scolded himself. He could not explain the strange urge that had taken hold of him, to show himself to her as though he expected her reaction to be different to anyone else's. The horror in her eyes when she'd seen his face…

Horror, but not fear, he reflected. At least that was something. And she had agreed to tour the island with him, which he had to admit had surprised him. He'd never taken anyone on a tour of Beacon Isle before. What would a lady wish to see?

He would ask…who? No one knew her. He didn't even know her name, for she'd meekly accepted the teasing moniker he'd thrown at her without a murmur. Yet a moment earlier, she'd been as fierce as a she-bear, calling him a pirate. Synonymous with scum...a lady of some education, then, who spoke her mind even as she read his own. For she'd known about his distaste for pirates, he was certain of it.

And for all his thirst for answers, she hadn't told him anything. He hadn't counted on her being so clever. For a woman so beautiful...it seemed almost too much that she had a mind to match.

He needed to spend more time with her. His idea to take her on a tour of the island had been a good one, he was certain, but he wanted more time before that, too. Time to set her at her ease, to persuade her that however hideous he looked, he was still a man of honour, and she would be safe beneath his roof. Safe enough to spill some of her secrets into his ear.

"I'll invite her to dinner!" he exclaimed.

"Very good, master," Inga said behind him.

He whirled. "How long have you been following me?"

"I have not left, master. After I undressed her, I waited outside in case I was needed. I hope you will change her mind about breaking the curse."

So Inga had heard everything, it seemed. Vardan wasn't surprised. "Any advice you'd care to offer me on that count? For I have yet to find a woman who can stare at someone as beastly as I am and not shudder in disgust."

"Love is not all about how one looks, master," Inga said reproachfully.

"Beasts don't love. Only men do that."

Inga grasped his arm. "And women. Don't forget that, master. Of all her children and grandchildren, the good Queen Margareta loved you best of all. She would want happiness for you. If you can win this lady's heart and break the curse, then – "

"Then men will fly, we will enjoy fresh strawberries every day, and King Thorn will declare that Beacon Isle is its own kingdom, to be ruled by what the ancients called a democracy, or a republic, or some other mythical name. Do not let your hopes rise too far, or their wings will melt and your spirits will fall so low you will have no hope left." Vardan closed his eyes. "I am sorry. This bitterness shall pass. I will set my hopes low: that she will one day look at me without disgust, and that she will share a meal with me."

"Invite her to supper, then, master, for if it is dark in the great hall, you can better hide in the shadows."

Vardan nodded sharply. "I shall. Who knows? Perhaps one day I will not need to hide."

Inga sounded sad. "I hope that day comes."

Fifteen

Zuleika waited until she was certain he was gone before she climbed out of bed and dressed. It wasn't until she realised she didn't know who had removed her clothes, she wondered whether he had done it. The laces she was trying to tie dropped from her numb fingers. No – surely not. The green woollen gown had been neatly folded in the chest, much like it was when she found it. A prince would not know how to fold gowns. Like his brother, he probably only knew how to tear them off helpless women.

No, her clothes had been cared for by one of the mysterious maids she had yet to meet. As if to prove a point, someone knocked tentatively at the door.

"My lady?" It was a woman's voice this time. "The master has supper served in the great hall. If you are feeling well enough, you are invited to join him." A pause. "But if you are still unwell, I shall bring a tray."

Zuleika was not so lazy as to wish to make extra work for the maids. "I will join him."

"Very good, my lady. Will you need my help to dress?"

Zuleika considered the laces she'd given up on. "No, I think I can manage." After all, she'd travelled to many places in the world without a maid, and managed to dress herself. But supper alone with the prince in the great hall... Now, that called for something a little more fancy than the green wool travelling dress she had chosen earlier. Instead, she chose a red velvet one, the colour of wine, much finer than the red dress she'd arrived in.

She took her time with the shell combs, knowing that the more beautiful she looked, the more information she could extract from the prince. For all his talk of a curse, no magic had touched the cargo. And where were the crew? If he had captured them and sold them as slaves...

Zuleika shook her head. If the man was a slaver, then he deserved his fate.

Instead of her boots, Zuleika chose a pair of soft slippers she found in the chest. They fitted her so well, it was almost as if they had been made for her. She felt a peculiar urge to dance. Later, she told herself. Once her investigations were finished, her father's cargo had been returned to him, and the man responsible for sinking his ships had tasted justice.

She needed no spell to guide her to the great hall this time, for she knew her way. A good thing, too, for it appeared that her lengthy preparations had made her late for dinner. The prince sat at one end of the long table, while a place was set for her at the opposite end. Platters of more food than two people could eat covered the wooden surface between them. When Zuleika sat down, she found the lighting so dim that she could scarcely see her food, let alone the man at the other end of the table.

"Do you normally eat in the dark, or do you simply dislike the sight of me?" Zuleika asked the prince.

He pretended not to hear her, though she was certain that he had.

Zuleika folded her arms across her breast. "I will not eat what I cannot see. I need more light."

Silence swelled for a moment between them, before the prince clapped his hands and called, "The Lady Belle demands more light. She wishes to see."

Zuleika heard the sharp intake of breath behind her, followed by scurrying feet. Perhaps the prince did like to eat in darkness. Minutes passed, before Zuleika heard the tramp of feet. Not one pair, like before, but a veritable army of servants, bearing light. When they came into view, it was her turn to gasp. For there were no servants in sight. All she could see was a row of lit candles, marching in midair. Yet she had heard the sound of feet on stone.

Djinn, was her first thought, or another enchantress like herself. "What is this magic?" she demanded.

The prince gestured at his hideous visage, now clearly visible in the bright illumination. "It is merely a part of my curse, Lady Belle," he said. "Not even the strongest man on the island wishes to share a meal with me, for one look at my face turns his stomach. I did not wish to ruin your appetite for supper. My cook may be invisible, but her sturgeon pie is the best in the region, if not the world."

Invisible servants. No wonder Zuleika hadn't seen her assailant. There had been nothing to see.

Reluctantly, Zuleika returned to her seat. She met the prince's eyes squarely across the length of the table. Though he looked hideous, more beast than human, his eyes were the exception. His eyes missed nothing, and right now they were evaluating her reaction to his enchanted servants. She refused to be found wanting. She tore her gaze from his mesmerising eyes, and surveyed the now well-lit table. "You recommend the sturgeon pie, you say? Then I must taste some."

Before she could work out which pie was the one in question, a pie-laden plate rose off the table and flew toward her. It stopped at her elbow. A respectful female voice asked, "How much would you like, my lady?"

Invisible servants, Zuleika reminded herself. Beside her stood an ordinary maid who simply had the misfortune to be invisible. Zuleika indicated a generous slice, which appeared to part itself from the rest of the pie before floating to her plate. Even for an enchantress, accustomed to using magic every day, it was disconcerting to see floating food. She forced herself to smile directly at the prince as she picked up a knife and cut herself a small portion of pie. She popped it into her mouth without dropping her gaze.

Her eyes widened in surprise as she realised the prince was right about his cook's skill. The sturgeon pie, with its mix of salt and spice, and perhaps even a little cheese, was indeed the best she had ever tasted. Zuleika hastened to scoop up another bite.

"What do you think, Lady Belle?" the prince asked.

Zuleika swallowed. "I think," she said carefully, "that your strongest men are weak indeed. I would gladly share a meal with a far more frightening man than you, if it meant more of that delicious pie. I have half a mind to try to steal your cook."

"My staff are loyal to me, even despite the curse.

You would have better luck trying to steal a casket of jewels from my storeroom, and you have seen how badly that turns out." His voice held a warning edge.

Stealing from one's host was a gross violation of the laws of hospitality, as Zuleika well knew. She lowered her gaze. "I meant no disrespect to your household, your Highness."

"Vardan," he corrected. "I am a merchant prince, more than a royal one. Yes, I rule this isle, but not because of my birth. To everyone else here, I am the Trade Master of Beacon Isle. From what little I know of you so far, Lady Belle, I suspect you call no man your master." He smiled in what appeared to be amusement, but his eyes held a challenge.

"In that, you are correct, Vardan," she said sweetly. "Will you tell me more about how you came to be cursed?"

Vardan's gaze wandered around the room. "You may go," he said, waving his hands.

If Zuleika closed her eyes, she could almost imagine the servants clearing the room, leaving her alone with the prince as the candles formed an honour guard down the length of the table between them. "How do you know they are all gone?" she asked. "Someone could be standing silently in the corner, and you would never know."

His enormous shoulders rose and fell in a

noncommittal shrug. "So it is true what they say, that there is no loyalty amongst thieves. Lady Belle, you betray yourself every time you open your mouth. Servants will listen to the master's private conversations, and mine will learn all my secrets whether I will it, or no. Loyalty is how I know they will keep their mouths shut about it outside my household. But what I will tell you this evening is no secret. In fact, they know the story so well that they will add their own details to it and I will not be able to get a word in. You will forgive me if I'm selfish enough to wish to keep your attention to myself. We get so few visitors here."

Zuleika felt his eyes on her again. "Then tell your tale, oh, selfish prince. Why are you cursed?"

He lifted his goblet and drank deeply from his wine. "Those are two different questions, but the answer to both is the same. In truth, I am not certain, but I shall tell you what I know." He took a deep breath, then continued, "As my brother's herald is my witness, I retired one night, an ordinary man in a household of ordinary servants. On the morrow, I awoke to a household in uproar. Every man, woman and child in my employ had been cursed with invisibility, and when I emerged from my chamber, I was as you see now. Why I became impossible to look at, instead of invisible like the rest, heaven only knows. The only person in the house to escape the curse was my brother's herald, Sir Ryder. He had recently brought me a name day gift from my brother, the king. He took ship the following morning, bearing a message to my brother, asking him to investigate this curse which had befallen us.

"Some time later, my brother's answer arrived. His inquiries revealed that I had offended a powerful witch, who would never lift the curse as long as she lived. His advice was to hunt the woman down and slay her."

"And did you?" Zuleika blurted out.

"What do you take me for?" the prince demanded. "I am no coward, slaughtering defenceless women, witch or no. And even if I were to dishonour myself so, I am still not stupid. The curse a witch casts with her dying breath is far more powerful than any she casts in life. Damn near unbreakable, or so I have heard. And it is not just me she would curse. The whole population of Beacon Isle depends on me to break the curse we are already under. So I sent another missive to my brother, asking him to bargain with her. What must I do in order for her to lift the curse? I offered wealth, lands, pledging myself to her service, but her answer was none of these. The witch said I had rejected her charms when she offered herself to me, and if she could not have me, then she would make me so hideous, so repulsive, that no one else could bear to look at me. She would lift the curse if I pledged my love for her, or if a woman, more beautiful than she, fell in love with me in my current form. As my honour will never abide the first, and no woman will look at me, the curse is no closer to being broken than on the day the witch cast it."

"So you plan to seduce me?" Zuleika asked.

The prince laughed so hard he nearly fell off his chair. "Good heavens, no! Perhaps some of the servants, especially the more romantically inclined maids, hope I will do so, but you are safe from me, Lady Belle. I am not my brother. I do not seduce maidens for my own pleasure."

"Then you're a better man than your brother," she said vehemently. "He deserves this curse, not you."

Vardan laughed softly this time. "Ah, he would never refuse a woman's affections. But if the witch were to appear before me now as a beautiful maiden like yourself, I would still choose the curse over dishonour for I would not dishonour her. So you see, I am not blameless in this matter."

"I still wish to help you, if I can," Zuleika ventured. "It sits ill with me to let a wicked witch have her way."

The prince inclined his head. "Tomorrow, I shall show you the rest of Beacon Isle, and you shall see the extent of her curse. Then perhaps you will see how pointless it is to oppose a witch so powerful."

"No witch is invincible," Zuleika said. She thought of her own brush with death, mere days ago, when she had nearly drowned. The prince's servants might well have saved her life bringing her in from the snow.

"Perhaps not," he agreed. He stretched his arms up behind his monstrous head, fixing his gaze on her. "Now, Lady Belle, I have satisfied your curiosity, while mine hungers for answers. It is time for you to tell me how you came to be lying in my rose garden."

Zuleika swallowed. "It is?"

Sixteen

Haltingly, she told a tale about being aboard her father's ship, before finding herself in the water. She fought not to weep as she described how close she had come to drowning, but still she continued, "And then I found myself in the snow, where your servants found me." She cast her eyes down and sipped from her goblet.

Rolf had made his suspicions clear. In his opinion, the girl had heard the rumours that Beacon Isle was haunted by the ghosts of those who had once lived here which kept everyone else away, but she'd dismissed them as mere stories. Vardan couldn't blame her for that – he did not believe in ghosts, either. So she'd come here to search for the treasures the pirates had left in their cavernous lairs around the island, Rolf had insisted. The very fact that when she woke, she'd headed straight for the cellars to steal something precious confirmed it in Rolf's eyes.

But not Vardan's. Oh, he admitted it was possible. But he'd searched the casket of jewels twice, and found nothing but the pretty purple stones. Of all the jewels in his cellar, they were perhaps the least valuable of the lot. Why choose that when she could have had gold or rubies or diamonds?

Unless she'd just taken something at random to prove to someone else that she'd found the lost ships' cargo. That certainly fitted with her arriving her by magical means. She must have had help from someone.

Yet he'd lifted her from the snow himself – he'd felt the weight of water in her clothes, and smelled the salt from the sea. He didn't doubt her sincerity now when she spoke of near drowning.

How, then, was she here? And why?

Vardan wanted to pound his fist on the table and demand answers, but the girl had evidently been through quite an ordeal. That she could tell him anything at all was a miracle in itself. So instead, he forced himself to soften his tone. "And you know nothing of who pulled you from the water, and brought you to my home?"

She paused to swallow more wine. "No, your Highness. I saw no one."

Not even when she'd arrived here, as his invisible servants had frightened her so much she'd fainted. For all her strength of character, he must remember that she'd not long since awoken from a swoon. She was as delicate as the first spring flowers that ventured through the melting snow. Precious. In need of protection.

His heart stuttered in his chest as her gaze met his. Unflinching. Without horror or fear. Merely...curiosity, he decided. Perhaps it took more to satisfy her than he'd realised.

"Ask it," he suggested.

Her eyes widened. "Ask what?"

"The question dancing on the tip of your tongue. The one burning in your mind. Ask it," he said.

"It has occurred to me that while I have eaten this pie, you have not touched it. Is that a part of your curse? That you cannot eat, or enjoy food?"

Vardan shook his head. "No."

"Then is it poisoned?"

Lady or no, Belle had far more knowledge of the criminal classes and political intrigue than any respectable woman should have. What kind of woman suspected her food might be poisoned?

"No." He rose from his chair, marched down the length of the table and broke off a piece of the pie. He ate the whole slice while he stood before her, then washed it down with a goblet of wine poured from the same flagon Greta had used to fill her cup. Not once did his eyes leave hers. Finally, he swallowed and said, "You are safe here, Lady Belle. My servants are loyal and would not poison my food, or yours, and I will not hurt you. You have my word of honour."

For a long moment, her eyes stared into his, reading his soul, or so it felt. "Are you truly as honourable as you say, Vardan?"

He felt the peculiar urge to take the girl in his arms and kiss her. But that would hardly be honourable. Perhaps another time, when she knew him better and had learned to trust him. And they had found a way to break the curse. Then he might be permitted to kiss her without her recoiling in horror. "I hope so," he said fervently, both in answer to her and his own unspoken desires.

Seventeen

Later that night, Zuleika tossed and turned in her bed,
knowing the prince hadn't believed her vague
description of how she'd found herself in the water
and then in the snow. She'd mentioned her father's
ship, though, which had seemed to satisfy him, at least
a little. When she told him the jewel casket she'd taken
from his storeroom contained amethysts her father
had bought for her, he'd grown suspicious. Now, she
found it hard not to laugh. He'd believed the part
about her being aboard a ship, which was a lie, but
when faced with the truth that the jewels were hers, he
didn't believe her. Men made so little sense.

She'd begun to discern expressions in that ghastly

face of his, too, almost as if he was human. Well, he probably was still human, despite whatever the jealous witch had changed him into. Why change him into some sort of hybrid between beast and man, anyway? A toad or a squirrel would have been fine, and much easier. And why curse his household along with him? That part made no sense at all. Surely she had not tried to seduce them in addition to their master.

Zuleika shook her head. She had stumbled upon the strangest, magical mystery she had ever encountered. Her good sense told her to find some bare earth or rock tomorrow and cast a portal home to her father, to tell him she'd found his cargo.

Except…she still didn't know how it had ended up here, nor how she'd transport it home. Vardan hadn't told her everything, either, she realised. He kept his secrets, just as she kept hers.

Perhaps if she toured the island with him, as he'd planned, she could persuade him to drop his guard and tell her the full story. Maybe even enough to allow her to lift his curse…

Not by falling in love with him, of course. She had more powerful means at her disposal that he knew nothing about, and she wanted to keep it that way. For all his trepidation against antagonising the other witch, Zuleika had little to fear from her. She was a fully-fledged enchantress who conquered djinn, for goodness' sake. A witch who wasted her power on complicated curses when simple ones would do would be no match for Zuleika.

If she defeated the witch and restored the prince and his household to their former state, he might be so grateful that he'd help her bring her father's merchandise home. Now that would be worth the delay.

With that settled, Zuleika drifted off to sleep.

Eighteen

A persistent tapping on the door woke Zuleika. With no windows in the room, it was difficult to tell the time. If it was Vardan trying to enter, he could tap until his fingers fell off. He spoke of honour and of being nothing like his brother, but words were cheap. When a man sole into a girl's chamber by night to have his way with her, then he showed his true mettle. Zuleika had locked and warded the door, so the only way in was if she allowed him entrance.

"Who is it?" she asked.

"It's Inga and Greta, m'lady. We brought your breakfast and fresh clothes for your journey."

Zuleika thought she recognised the voice. "Did you

find me in the snow?"

"That was me, m'lady. I needed help to carry you in, before I shooed the menfolk out so I could take off your wet things. Your beautiful dress was ruined by the water, so we brought you something new."

Zuleika climbed out of bed and unbarred the door. She blinked for a moment as the corridor outside appeared empty, before she remembered the curse. "I can't see you, but you're still here, right?"

"Yes, my lady," the voice said, somewhere to Zuleika's left. Right above the floating breakfast tray. "You need not fear us. We're just ordinary women, the same as those in your household. You can't see us, what with the curse and all, but we'll make extra noise so you can hear us, and if you see things floating, that's because we're carrying them."

Zuleika stepped aside to let the tray, and presumably the woman carrying it, into the room. A second set of steps shuffled in behind the first woman.

"I have your clothes, my lady," a nervous voice said.

Unlike the breakfast tray, Zuleika couldn't see any clothes. "Where?" she asked.

"I'm carrying them in my arms, my lady. I will lay them out, so you can see them." True to her word, the girl shuffled over to the bed, where a blue gown materialised from thin air as it spread across the chest. "It's the master's favourite colour, my lady. He won't be able to take his eyes off you when you wear this."

Zuleika suppressed an unladylike snort. "You expect me to seduce your prince to break the curse? I'm not sure it works like that."

"But if he falls in love with you, and he won't be able to help himself, he will be the most charming prince imaginable. One you won't be able to help but fall in love with," the girl said dreamily.

"Greta's head is turned at the thought of all this romance, but she is right about the master. He is charming when he wants to be, and a good man, besides. We know why the witch cursed us as well as him. She knew we'd do everything humanly possible to help him break the curse. There are far worse men in this world than Prince Vardan, my lady. He is a rose among thorns, and no mistake." The older woman set the breakfast tray on the table beside the bed, as if to emphasise her point.

"You both believe I can break this curse," Zuleika marvelled. "What if the king is wrong, and the witch left no such loophole to break the spell? What then?"

The bed creaked as a depression appeared in the mattress, as though a heavy weight had settled on the edge. "Then my heart will break long before the master's. I have buried two children since the affliction turned us invisible. Two children whose faces I never saw, between birth and death. What fate is that for a child, to never see his mother's face, to never see a single smile?" Inga's voice shook with unseen tears. "My lady, I love the master as if he were my own son, and if bringing him happiness would let me see the face of my children once more, I would do anything. I beg you, if there is even the smallest kernel of compassion in you, help the master to break the curse."

A tear slipped down Zuleika's cheek. She could not refuse a mother's heartfelt plea. "I shall do whatever I can to help," she promised the woman.

Plump hands seized Zuleika's. "Thank you, my lady. And in return, I will help you. When the master sees you today, you will look like a queen."

"A princess, at best," Zuleika corrected. "You are not trying to tempt the king."

"A queen," Inga repeated firmly. "We want you to look too good for the master, so that he tries his hardest to win your heart. If you had only seen him before the curse, you would understand why a witch would want him for herself. He was the handsomest prince ever born. Why, even the king himself was jealous of him."

Zuleika reached for her loaf of bread and nibbled on the end. "Very well. Where do we start?"

"With the queen's jewels."

Zuleika choked. "The king's mother is here?"

Inga laughed, and even Greta tittered.

"No, my lady. Not Queen Katerina. The master's grandmother, Dowager Queen Margareta. This was her chamber, and the gown you wore to dinner last night was first worn by Her Majesty at her son's coronation. I can show you the coronation tapestry, if you like. She sewed it herself, so it shows the detail of the dress quite clearly."

Last night she had dressed like a queen. No wonder Vardan had stared at her so. Wearing his grandmother's dress, no less.

"You sound like my father." Zuleika sighed. "His ship carried silk and jewels and fur to make me a court dress so that I might tempt the king into marriage."

"They belong to your father?"

Present tense, not past, Zuleika noted. She nodded.

"I will speak to the seamstress. If the cloth is yours, perhaps she can make something of it. If you help his brother to break the curse, perhaps the king will be so grateful that —"

"NO!" Zuleika interrupted, louder than she'd intended. She hurried to explain, "If I break the curse, as you say, I will be in love with the prince. The king can look elsewhere for a bride." Or a whore, she thought but didn't say.

"Yes, my lady."

Though she couldn't see Inga's face, Zuleika was

certain the woman was smiling.

Nineteen

After enduring an interminably long toilette, Zuleika was finally allowed to make her way to the great hall, where she was told the prince waited for her. He had evidently grown impatient, for he was nowhere to be seen when she arrived. The heavy doors had been thrown open, so she ventured outside in search of him. The yard she entered sounded like it was full of people, but she could only see one – the prince. He stood in deep conversation with someone unseen, beside a magnificent dark horse. Yes, only a prince would own such an animal.

Zuleika gave the stallion a wide berth, as she made her way across the icy cobbles. The mare she presumed would be her mount seemed supremely unconcerned by the invisible people saddling her for the coming ride. Zuleika pulled off her glove and allowed the mare's misty breath to warm her hand, giving the horse her scent. "What is her name?" she asked the groom she knew to be in earshot.

"You are asking me, my lady?" At Zuleika's nod the man continued, "The master called her Embarr, on account of her swimming ashore from a shipwreck all by herself."

Zuleika nodded. The horse was yet another piece of the puzzle, for if she had come from a ship, she did not truly belong to the prince. "I think she shall suit me well indeed, provided she does not try to walk on water again."

The old man chuckled, which ended in a hacking cough. "Beg pardon, my lady. But Embarr here will not go near the water, not even to walk along the beach."

"Then she is a wise animal." Zuleika mounted the mare, aware of every eye upon her, including the prince's. She smoothed her skirts as he approached.

"Good morning, Lady Belle," he said. "Your beauty outshines the sun today."

Soft, feminine laughter floated out of the open door. Greta, Inga and several more, by the sound of it.

The girl she once was would have blushed. Zuleika

the enchantress merely smiled.

The prince moved in close, and stroked the mare's neck. He dropped his voice so low it was barely audible as he said, "They will stop at nothing, won't they? I'd wager there isn't a member of my household not watching us now."

Zuleika ducked her head. In a low voice, she replied, "I believe you're right, your Highness. After all, they stand to gain much if the curse is broken."

His voice rumbled in his throat. "And yet they have made you irresistible. If the witch who cursed me had looked like you do now, I could not have refused her anything. Do you think they would cheer if I were to throw you to the ground right now, and ravish you here before them?"

It sounded like a jest, but the look in his eyes was too intense for levity.

Zuleika stiffened. "I think you would disappoint them. They believe they serve a good, honourable man. Not a beast who ruts with unwilling women."

A wolf. That was what he reminded her of right now. Something about him unsettled the mare, too. Zuleika nudged the horse forward through the gate.

"Make haste, your Highness," she called over her shoulder. "It is discourteous to keep a lady waiting."

She allowed Embarr to continue walking, until the clatter of hooves brought the prince to her side. She opened her mouth to say something else, but she closed it with a snap as they stepped out of the shelter of the high wall. The prince's house perched on a hill, overlooking the town and what must have been the harbour. The water was empty of ships today, though. If the prince owned all this, he was a wealthy man, with no need to resort to piracy.

She glanced at the prince, and found his eyes still fixed on her.

Before she could look away, he said, "I must apologise. I meant no disrespect. What I said, I said in jest. No more. My brother always said I had a fey sense of humour. I only wished to set you at ease in front of our audience, and instead I... I am sorry."

"If a man can jest about ravishing women, then what is to stop him following words with action? I assure you, rape is no joke, your Highness."

He seized Embarr's bridle, forcing her to stop. "I made a mistake, and offered you my apology. You are correct that rape is no joke. But you are wrong if you believe that words said in jest are no different to a man's actions. I have never forced a woman, and I will not. I am not a beast. Whether you believe it or not, you need not fear me. I will not hurt you, Lady Belle."

She wanted to drop her gaze, but found she could not. No beast had ever looked so earnest. She wished she could believe him, if only for the sake of his household. She sighed. "Then perhaps we should start again. I shall bid you good morning, and ask whether you slept well?"

He released the mare's bridle as he relaxed. "It is a fine winter morning for a ride. I wish I had slept better, but a mysterious maiden danced through my dreams, disturbing my slumber with her secrets."

More flattery. "Ah, dancing maidens can be quite troublesome. I find it best to let them dance until they are exhausted, so that they fall asleep on their own, and leave you to rest."

The prince snorted softly. "So the maiden sleeps, but not I? That will not do. In order to sleep, I must dance, too."

A faint smile touched Zuleika's lips. "Then you must try it tonight, or the next time the maiden invades your dreams, your Highness, and let me know whether it works for you."

"Vardan," he corrected. "I am no one's Highness here. And as I have no doubt she will return tonight, if she permits me to dance with her, I shall give you a full report in the morning."

She laughed aloud. "As long as all you do is dance, your report will be fit for a lady's ears."

He grinned, showing more pointed teeth than any man should. "That I cannot promise. I am a man, after all."

Yes. She could not afford to forget that.

"A man who rides a rather splendid horse. I have no doubt he has an equally splendid name. Bucephalus, perhaps?" she asked.

"No, I am no general, and I have no desire to conquer the world. His name is Arion."

She nodded. "The speedy steed of the sea king. More noble still."

"A gift from my brother. He came on the last ship to enter the harbour before we were cursed." Vardan reined in his horse and pointed. "You see those rocks there? The ones that look like fangs? That's where the entrance to the harbour used to be. Now, we can't even get a fishing boat out at high tide."

That explained the absence of ships in port. "How did you get the ship out, then?" Zuleika asked, puzzled. "You say it entered the harbour, but there are no ships here now. How did it get out?"

He stared at her for a long moment before he answered, "By road. We built an enormous cart, harnessed every pony on the island to it, and rolled it from the harbour to the sea. It was all for naught, though, for it hadn't even sailed out of sight before she ran into another patch of rocks the lookout never saw until it was too late. Tore out the bottom of her hull and she sank like a stone. Most of the crew drowned, and those that did not...returned to port in their boats to spread stories of what they called Haunted Isle, not Beacon Isle, on account of the ghosts."

Zuleika blinked. "You have ghosts, too?"

He hesitated. "No, but...you shall soon see." He spurred Arion on, toward the town.

Curious, Zuleika followed.

Twenty

Either she was as practiced at pretence as the craftiest courtier, or Belle truly did not know about the island's haunted reputation. But how could she have heard about the island's treasures without hearing the ghost stories?

She had refused to wear any of his grandmother's jewels, too – which made her a strange thief. The casket of gems she'd tried to steal were worth far less than one of Queen Margareta's diamond or pearl necklaces. Yet Inga said Belle had done little more than touch the treasures before declaring them impractical for riding, and asked Inga to return them to the locked chest where they normally resided.

Only a peculiar woman indeed could resist Queen Margareta's jewels.

Yet she had not refused the horse. Embarr was not as spirited a creature as Arion, but she was a horse bred for royalty. She seemed to accept Belle quite happily, and the lady's seat showed her a practiced horsewoman. Either her thievery ran to horses, or the lady kept a fine stable.

But if she was a member of the high nobility as she appeared, her manners were not those of a noble maiden, or at least not the women he'd met at court. She was courteous enough, but she did not bow her head in humility like most girls did. No, she held his gaze with considerable pride. She would never be any man's obedient wife, he thought, fighting down laughter at the thought. Should her father marry her to a weak man, she would undoubtedly turn into a shrew. But if she chose her own husband – and she certainly appeared old enough to be in her majority, and able to choose – she deserved someone who would continue to light that fire in her eyes that made them sparkle so. A woman such as her should never be broken by a bad husband.

If only he were in a position to ask for her hand...but what woman would accept him, looking the way he did? Even Belle with her piercing gaze would never see past the beast he'd become.

Twenty-One

Vardan slowed Arion down to a walk when they reached the first building. Zuleika followed suit. "Welcome to Harbourtown," Vardan said, spreading his arms wide. "A ghost town, now."

And so it looked, for not a soul was in sight. A pony plodded down the middle of the cobblestone street, pulling a laden cart. A cat dashed between the wheels and emerged unscathed. Spray of snow fountained up from the drift by the side of the road, as though a child had kicked it. As though...

Zuleika dismounted, wrapping the reins around her hand so she didn't lose Embarr in the crowd. A crowd she could not see, but she could hear.

The witch hadn't just cursed the prince's household. She'd cursed an entire town, bustling with people and businesses and all the things a place of this size should have. Even Zuleika couldn't cast a curse this far-reaching. No single spell-caster had done this. She would have had to cast dozens of curses to enchant this many people. It was...inconceivable that one witch would expend so much power to punish one man.

Zuleika moved in a daze, not looking where she was going, and she stumbled. She would have fallen, if not for her hold on the horse's reins. As it was, she landed painfully on her knees, tearing one of the lovely silk stockings Inga had insisted she wear. Now, the blue silk was stained purple with her blood.

Before she could think the action through, Zuleika touched her bloodied knee to the cobbles. "Show me what the curse hides," she whispered. She watched the spell eddy down the street as if blown by the wind, and as it went, people faded into sight. Men, women, children, going about their business as though there was no curse. But that wasn't right, either. The women's veils were crooked, for they could not see to set them straight. The children's hair was mussed, because no one ever saw it to admonish them to brush it. Two men stood outside the baker's in stained tunics, blissfully unaware of their need to wash. The people of

Harbourtown weren't only invisible to the world. They were invisible to themselves, too.

Before her eyes, children lived without ever seeing their mother's loving smile. Just as Inga had said.

Tears sprang to Zuleika's eyes. She must fix this. There had to be a way.

Strong hands seized her, lifting her to her feet.

"Are you all right?" Vardan asked, not taking his arms from around her.

The townsfolk stopped to stare. At their prince, with a strange woman in his arms. Realisation dawned on their faces, as men began to bow and women dropped curtseys.

"I am fine," Zuleika tried to say, turning her head so that she might see his face, but the words died in her throat. The beastly face – Vardan's face – that she expected to see was not there. Instead, she saw the face of King Thorn, an unspeakable monster she would never allow to touch her again.

She closed her eyes and released her hold on the spell, which dispersed its magic in a cloud of tiny stars only she could see. Zuleika dared to open her eyes, and breathed a sigh of relief as she saw Vardan's hideous visage once more. Unable to help herself, she lifted a hand to his cheek. It felt...smooth, like the skin of a man, and not a beast. The curse on him was merely illusion, she realised. Underneath it, he looked like...a beast.

Zuleika wrenched herself out of his grasp and straightened her cloak. "I am fine," she said finally, unwilling to look at him now. "I did not look where I was going."

"Perhaps you should stay on your horse. Her hooves are more sure than your feet."

Flushing with embarrassment, Zuleika climbed back on the mare. She knew he'd seen it, that moment of panic as she was helpless in a man's arms again. A man who looked like him, if only for a moment. "He is not his brother," she told herself. One glance at the prince confirmed it. How strange. The monstrous face she'd shied away from before was now a relief to look upon.

She met his eyes. Not his brother at all. "I think you are right." She swallowed, then continued, "Please, show me the town. I would like to see everything I can. I didn't realise the curse stretched so far. Whoever this witch is, she must be stopped."

Murmurs of agreement came from the townspeople lining the road.

"My brother told me her name. Something foreign, it sounded like. Zulu or Zollie or…"

"Zuleika?" she said, feeling sick.

Vardan nodded. "Something like that. He said if I didn't have the stomach to slay her, I should send her to him instead, and he would do the deed."

She should have killed the king instead of simply cursing him. Blaming her for a curse this huge? Zuleika had never met this man before, let alone tried to seduce him, and she'd certainly never cursed an entire town in a fit of pique.

"What did you tell him?" Zuleika didn't like the way her voice shook.

"That if he wants a woman, he can hunt her down himself. Beacon Isle is my responsibility, now more than ever. Do you not agree?"

Numbly, Zuleika nodded.

But inside, she felt far too much. The king was hunting her, he'd said. How far would he go to find her? A man with no honour might do anything, including breaking promises he never intended to keep. He might even hurt her family…

"You do not look well, Lady Belle. Perhaps you should rest a moment in the inn, and take some refreshment. Harbourtown's hospitality has earned it quite a reputation. The ships might not dock here anymore, but the innkeeper has not changed."

She allowed Vardan to help her off her horse and into the dim interior of the inn. People fussed around her, but all she could see was Vardan's eyes, filled with concern for her.

No, she was not the one in danger. Her father was,

and somehow, she had to warn him.

Twenty-Two

The innkeeper settled Zuleika in a chair beside the fire while Vardan called for the speciality of the house.

"This is the best inn in Harbourtown, you'll see," Vardan told her. "Farlof's brother, Karl, has the largest farm on the southern part of the isle. If we're lucky, he might still have some of that dewberry wine." He cupped his hands to his mouth. "Ho! Elena! The lady wants wine!"

Zuleika frowned at him. "I said no such thing."

"Ah, you will once you taste it, my lady," a female voice said, before a tray floated into the room. "His Highness knows what he's about. When he was a boy visiting his grandmother on the island, you could tell the time by him. He'd be on my doorstep the moment the baking was out of the oven. And he still has a taste for them. That's the secret to why he chose to live at Beacon Isle and not the capital with the king. Saffron buns washed down with the island's own dewberry wine will be enough to make you want to stay forever."

Saffron buns? Zuleika had not tasted the spice more than once or twice in her life, but the curlicued cakes on the tray did look quite yellow, even in the dim light. And she could smell them — they must be still warm from the oven. Her mouth watered, but she didn't dare take one before the prince. She might be dressed like a queen, but she knew all too well he was far higher than she would ever be in the social pecking order. Royalty ate first. Always.

"Take one, my lady," Elena urged.

"After five years living under this curse, they see one pretty girl and forget I'm a prince," Vardan grumbled. "On Beacon Isle today, the woman who could break the curse ranks higher than royalty. How the mighty have fallen." He shook his head, but his eyes held amusement.

Still Zuleika hesitated.

"Oh, by all that's holy." Vardan seized a pastry and held it to her lips. "Bite, Lady Belle, and I promise you, you'll fall in love."

She blinked, but there was nothing magical about

the cakes. No hidden love spell. Nothing but the buttery, spicy aroma that tempted her to…

Zuleika bit into the pastry, as cheering erupted from the prince. She took it from his fingers as she chewed the morsel. The saffron bun was every bit as good as it smelled. Light and crisp and just the slightest bit sweet. Before she'd realised it, she'd finished the whole thing.

Not even Vardan had made such a pig of himself – he was only halfway through his bun. "What is your verdict, Lady Belle?"

"The cakes are lovely," she said. "But I thought you said you were an honourable man. You are trying to seduce me with food."

"And wine!" he added, filling a cup and holding it out to her. "Don't forget the wine."

She took the cup, but she didn't drink. "You didn't answer me, your Highness."

"Vardan, and I believe I did. Food and wine, the best we have to offer, for my guest. There is nothing dishonourable in offering hospitality to a beautiful lady."

Zuleika heard shuffling footsteps, like someone trying to leave the room as quietly as possible. She stared into the depths of her wine cup in order to avoid his soul-piercing eyes. "But you are trying to seduce me."

"If there is a way to help my people and retain my honour, I will do what I must. If all I succeed in doing is to make you fall in love with Beacon Isle, as I have, then so be it. You are welcome to stay."

On a cursed island where the invisible people would be a daily reminder that there was a more powerful witch than her who worked for the king and was willing to blame her for inflicting this horror on the island. While her father worried.

Zuleika shook her head. "My father will be waiting for news of his lost ship. I must return home. Once you have shown and told me all you can about this curse, perhaps I can look in my mother's library at home for ways to break it." She drank the wine. Elena was right about her wanting more.

"First, you should check our library here. I'm sure it's far superior to anything your mother may have collected. My house used to be a monastery. The monks refused to stay in a building suffering under a curse, so they left, but they could not take everything. I'll show you on our return."

A monastery library wouldn't contain much about magic, but Zuleika held her tongue. She was fond of reading, and she would relish the chance to see his collection. He already knew two of her weaknesses — good food and wine. She didn't dare let him add a third: reading.

After all, she still didn't know how he'd come to be in possession of her father's goods. Or why the witch had chosen to target him for her curse. For all his talk of honour, there had to be something wrong with the man to justify such a punishment.

Either that, or she was missing something that might help her make sense of all this. She knew she wouldn't find the answer in any library, though – Vardan held the key to the curse, she was certain of it. How to extract it…she did not know. But she would enjoy finding out.

Twenty-Three

When Vardan was certain Belle had rested sufficiently – and they'd eaten all of Elena's saffron cakes, which was only to be expected – he suggested they continue on the tour.

He read her hesitation in her eyes – such a marvellous thing, to see another person's expression again! Her face was both delightful and expressive, a treat to observe – and offered, "Or we could remain here at the inn and resume the tour on the morrow, when you are better rested. We could return to my house, if you no longer wish to..." No longer wish to see any more of me or my island, he tried to say, but the words stuck in his throat.

She'd looked at him with such horror and fear on the road outside that he'd nearly dropped to his knees under the weight of his despair. Could he have imagined the other times she'd looked at him and seen more than just a beast? Because the sheer intensity of the terror in her eyes for that moment had been enough to unman him. She hadn't been the only one in need of some wine when they entered the inn.

Yet she'd reached up to touch his face, and her terror had vanished. No one had touched him like that in a very long time. Like she actually wanted to.

A whisper of hope sent a shiver through his soul. Perhaps the curse could be broken by Lady Belle.

She rose and smoothed her skirt before reaching for her cloak. "I fear if I rest any longer, I shall fall asleep. I ate far too many of those delicious cakes. A ride in the crisp winter air should wake me up nicely." She paused. "Unless you are too tired of my company to continue, of course. I cannot have a tour of this island without a suitable guide."

Yes, she had recovered, Vardan decided, hurrying to fasten his cloak so he could follow her outside.

"I'll bring the next batch out in a basket, Prince Vardan," Elena said. "And some wine. Your lady will want more, and so will you. Winning a lady's heart is hard work."

"You think I can win it, too?" Vardan asked

bitterly. "Is there anyone on this cursed island who I will not disappoint when I fail?"

"I know some cheeky lads who like being invisible, so they can cause more mischief, but a good clout around the ears will sort them out. It certainly worked on you when you were a boy." Though he couldn't see it, Vardan knew she was smiling. Elena continued, "She has a playful heart, that one. I warrant she would dearly love to dance with the right man."

A man, and not a beast. Vardan sighed.

"The cakes you wanted, ma'am," said a younger voice.

Elena made an irritated sound in her throat. "Give them to the prince, then!"

The girl thrust the basket hard against Vardan's midsection. "There you go."

"Your Highness," Elena reminded her.

"There you go, your Highness," the girl said sulkily. Stomping footsteps signified that she'd left.

"The sooner you break this curse, the better," Elena said with feeling.

Vardan bowed his head. "I will do all that honour permits."

"Don't forget the wine. It's in the basket, with the cakes."

Vardan nodded his thanks and carried his burden out to Arion.

He felt Belle's eyes on him as he secured the basket to his saddle. He mounted before he said, "Are you ready to see more of my domain, Lady Belle?"

She took a deep breath, closing her eyes in appreciation. "If that's another basket of those cakes you're carrying, I might just follow you anywhere."

Vardan offered up an earnest prayer that her words were more than jest. "They are," he said shortly. "So let's go." He set off at a walk, hearing the clop of Embarr's hooves following behind.

Twenty-Four

The buildings lining the harbour were a mixture of storehouses and taverns. Though she had never entered one, Zuleika recognised some of the waterside buildings as brothels. Many of the taverns were not yet open, for which she blamed the early hour, but the brothels never closed. Idly, she wondered if they did better business with invisible clientele. She considered asking Vardan, but a prince had no need to frequent a common whorehouse when he could follow his brother's example and turn his subjects into whores for his own private use. She sighed, only half listening as the prince told her how all the storehouses in Harbourtown were full, which was why he'd started to store goods in his cellars.

"Can't you just sell things?" Zuleika blurted out. "Full storehouses breed vermin, and goods can be damaged when they are stored too long. Especially foodstuffs. If they are full of the same things as your cellars, they are trade goods. Their value is not in being stockpiled, but in being sold to the right market, or so my father says."

Vardan nodded. "Your father is correct. But who would we sell them to, Lady Belle?" He waved his hand at the empty harbour. "There are no ships. No traders from east or west, though we used to welcome them daily. And if my people approach shore in their fishing boats, no one sees them. Others try to steal their goods, thinking the boats are empty, and no one wishes to trade with a ghost. Or me."

She hadn't thought of that, but Zuleika supposed it made sense. Still... "How do the trade goods arrive here if not by ship?"

"This is not our only harbour," Vardan replied. "Beacon Isle is bigger than you might think."

It still didn't add up in Zuleika's head. "But if there are other harbours, why are the goods not stored there, near the ships? And if you can transport goods from the other harbour to this one, why can't you send some of this cargo out on the ships when they leave?"

"There are no ships," he repeated.

"Why not?" she persisted.

"Pirates, and the curse, though we've found the curse quite convenient when it comes to combating pirates," Vardan said with a smile.

Zuleika was intrigued. "No one wins against pirates, or so my father says. They sail away to their secret bases, sell slaves and all their stolen merchandise, and live high until they find another ship to prey upon. They cannot be stopped, for as long as the secret bases remain and one man knows how to reach them, there will always be men willing to become pirates."

Vardan laughed. "Now that's where you're wrong. Let me show you."

Zuleika didn't understand her hesitation. Wasn't he offering her the knowledge she wanted? She mentally shook herself before she said, "All right. Show me."

Twenty-Five

Vardan guided Arion up to the cliff path, glancing back over his shoulder every now and again to make sure Lady Belle still followed him. He was worried about her swooning again, he told himself. Not admiring the purple fire in her eyes that kindled into life the moment they reached the clifftops.

For a woman who had almost drowned, she showed surprisingly little fear of the ocean. In fact, she seemed almost exhilarated by the stiff breeze whipping the sea into waves that boomed like battering rams when they struck the base of the cliffs. Or maybe it was the way the breeze plucked her hair from its braids and turned the silky strands into curls.

No wonder women kept their hair covered under veils. Unfettered, hers was…mesmerising. Once again, he wanted to reach out and stroke it. But he wouldn't, because to see her cringe away again would be another dagger to his heart. Once the curse was lifted, then she might look upon him with something that wasn't horror. Had all the islanders looked at him in the same way since the curse took effect? If so, perhaps their invisibility was a blessing and not a curse for him.

If the witch who cursed him planned things that way, she could hardly be the cold-hearted bitch his brother had said she was. For the first time since she cursed him, Vardan wanted to meet the woman. Or meet her again, as he'd evidently already met her but couldn't recall her. Why couldn't the witch have looked like Lady Belle, for he'd never forget a face or figure like hers. But even if she had, honour would have demanded he resist her advances.

Unless she'd looked like Lady Belle and he wanted to make her his wife.

He snorted. He'd known the girl for barely a day. He shouldn't be considering the possibility of marriage to her, or all that it entailed. Vardan owned that he had little control over his dreams, and the fact that she had been the maiden dancing naked through them did not mean he should be imagining undressing her now.

The lady's voice cut through his daydream. "You

have the most peculiar smile on your face. Is there something special about this place, that it should inflame you with such love?"

You, Vardan thought but didn't say as he felt blood heat his cheeks. He doubted she would see it, though, for beasts did not blush.

"Yes," he said finally. "This is where I show you how one man with the knowledge of secret pirate bases can win against them all." He swung down from his horse, indicating that she should do the same. "We'll go on foot from here."

Lady Belle slid down gracefully, her boots barely making a sound as they landed on the windswept rock. The salt wind kept the cliffs free of snow through all but the coldest winters. "To where, precisely?" She tucked a wayward curl behind her ear.

What was it about her hair that distracted him so? Vardan shook his head. "Why, to the pirates' lair, of course." He laughed at her puzzled expression, and drew her to the very edge of the cliffs so he could point. "The cliffs along the northern side of the island are riddled with caves just like that one. And for a long time, pirates used these to store their stolen cargo. Some are even big enough to sail a ship inside."

"Truly?" Her eyes danced.

"Truly," he replied. "I will show you." He took her hand and pulled her to the very brink on the cliff.

Lady Belle balked, much like Embarr did when faced with the ocean waves. The horse nibbled at some of the hardy plants that had sprouted between the rocks, unconcerned, as her mistress dug her heels in with astonishing strength. "Unless you can fly, your Highness, there is no way you're taking me over that cliff. I like living, thank you."

He sighed. Reluctantly, he released her hand. "There are steps. See?" Vardan stepped over the edge and down the first three stone steps, worn smooth by wind, wave and the passage of many feet.

She blinked in surprise. "Down the entire cliffside?" Lady Belle swallowed, her eyes wide. "I may need your arm after all." Her hand was warm as she grasped his.

Vardan brought her fingers to his lips and kissed them lightly without thinking. Thank heaven she didn't pull away before he realised his mistake. "My apologies, Lady Belle."

"No need to apologise. I may not be accustomed to descending from clifftops, but I rarely require a man's arm to walk." She proceeded to demonstrate that she was as surefooted as her horse as she followed Vardan down the winding steps to the cave.

The steps ended at a narrow stone ledge which at high tide was washed by the waves. Now, it was simply damp with spray and strewn with seaweed thrown up in the last storm. And slippery. "Be careful here, Lady

Belle," he said, glancing behind to make sure she did not lose her footing. She'd hoisted her skirts a little to better see her feet, but Vardan glimpsed a shapely ankle and found himself longing to see more. Perhaps even the naked maiden of his dreams.

His trod hard on a piece of seaweed, and his foot shot forward, throwing him backward into her arms. His face ended up pressed against her breast for one delightful moment before he came to his senses and righted himself, repeating his profuse apologies.

Lady Belle did not seem inclined to forgive him. "As you say, Vardan. Do be careful." She did not take his hand again.

Sighing, he led the way.

Twenty-Six

It was panic that made her heart beat wildly when Vardan fell against her, Zuleika told herself. With his face pressed against her breast, he probably heard it through all the layers of fabric between them. The flush of heat she'd felt was mortification at being so close to a man, a man who looked like he did under the curse, as she well knew.

And there was a tingle of something more when he touched her, too. Something magical, that had nothing to do with being touched by a man. The magic that hummed so powerfully through him felt familiar, as though it liked her. She'd never felt anything like it. Magic didn't have feelings, or preferences for people.

Yet each spell contained a little of the essence of its caster, because it was the caster's blood that fuelled the spell. Each essence was as individual as the caster, and this…this was not new to her. She must know the witch who had cursed Vardan.

Except that she didn't know many witches, particularly one whose magic was so dark it had no colour at all except black, for this curse appeared like a shadow across the island. The few witches she had met in her travels were mostly enslaved djinn, whose magic she'd needed to undo. Their magic naturally recognised her as an adversary, and buzzed with alarm at her approach. Vardan's curse seemed to hum with welcome.

No witch had ever welcomed her. Except her mother, of course, but her mother had lain in her grave these six years at least. Longer than Vardan had been cursed, so she couldn't have cast this enchantment.

Zuleika's hands itched to touch the prince again, to investigate the curse upon him more thoroughly. She forced her arms to stay by her sides. He was no different to his brother, and being overly familiar with him would not turn out well. She did not want to touch a man, nor have him touch her. Ever.

She ducked under a low overhang and stepped into darkness.

Steel scraped across flint, and a moment later a torch flared into life. Instead of orange, this flame was the colour of bluebells.

"More magic?" Zuleika asked.

Vardan's eyes seemed to glow in the firelight. "We have no witches on the island, and none who are generous enough to use their magic to light the caves. Had we even a single witch, I would have asked her to help break the curse. No, these are driftwood torches, soaked in salt water. 'Tis the salt that burns blue." Vardan eyed her suspiciously. "Why such fear for magic, Lady Belle? Do you suffer from a curse, too?"

Zuleika choked back a laugh. Cursebreaking was her specialty. Not even the most powerful djinn could keep a curse focussed on her for long. "I do not fear magic," she managed to say. "But this island is already enchanted in ways I have never seen before. To a witch who could make a whole town invisible, I'm sure a little light is nothing."

Vardan nodded, as though he accepted her explanation. He held the torch aloft as he stepped out of the narrow passage. "This is the main cavern."

Zuleika gasped as the cave opened out into a space that could have held the cathedral in the capital, so large was it. The floor stretched away into the darkness, outside of their circle of light, and behind her she could hear the splash of waves as the ocean made its presence known, though she could not see the water.

"This cavern is big enough to sail into when the tide is not too high, which is why it was a favourite among the local pirate fleet. They waited here until a rider from town told them a particularly rich cargo was leaving the harbour, and they'd venture out under cover of darkness to attack the unsuspecting vessel. Often, they unloaded their ill-gotten gains here so they could return for them and trade them in town, sometimes to the same merchants they'd stolen them from. I've known the same pelts to appear in the market no less than six times, sold to a new merchant only for it to be stolen again. Quite ingenious, really." Vardan smiled grimly. "Or it was, until I became Trade Master of Beacon Isle."

"So you discovered their ploy?" Zuleika guessed.

Vardan shrugged. "No, I can't take full credit for that. My steward, Rolf, suspected something like it, but it wasn't until the curse took effect that we knew for certain. You see, we changed overnight, and when the next day dawned, we were all as you see now. The pirates, however, were unchanged. Usually, they brought their stolen cargo from the caves by cart, working in the middle of the night to make sure no one saw them arrive or leave as they stocked their storehouses by the harbour. The morning they returned to trade...they entered a market empty of people. Or so they thought." He chuckled. "The panic had died down, so the villagers watched in invisible rage as some of their own, traitors that they had trusted, walked into town untouched by the curse. When they saw the town empty, they raced back to the cave...but not alone. Many followed them back to the pirate lair. Now, these pirates did not just steal cargo. Oh, no. They also sold the crews as slaves. Many townspeople had family members who had served as sailors, and no small number of these were enslaved by pirates. So what ensued in this cave...I can only describe as a bloodbath. The pirates were no match for their invisible, furious foes. There were no survivors."

Part of Zuleika recoiled in horror at the thought of the violence Vardan described, but a larger part of her revelled in triumph at the victory. For surely some of the enslaved crews had been her father's men. And the pirates' booty... "What of the stolen cargoes?" she asked.

"What, no tears for the dead men, slaughtered right here where they stood?" Vardan asked, spreading his arms wide.

"Pirates are scum. Exterminating such vermin is a public service, I am sure. But what of the treasures stored here?"

If her all of her father's missing merchandise was

still on the island somewhere, then all was not lost.

"Locked in my storehouses, secure and waiting for their rightful owners' return, Lady Thief," Vardan replied. "Look all you like. You will find no pirate treasures here."

Why did he not understand? "I am no thief," she said steadily, looking him in the eye. "And I begin to believe that neither are you. But it beggars belief that all the goods in your cellars and storehouses were once stored in this cave. Either it is bigger than it looks, or it was stacked to the very roof."

"This cave stretches for miles beneath the island, so it most certainly is bigger than it first appears. But you are correct. Not all the goods in my house or the whole of Harbourtown came from the pirate stash here."

Zuleika found herself nodding. "Like the cargo from the *Rosa*. She was only lost a few weeks ago, a month at most. Long after you cleaned out this pirate lair. How, then, came all the goods to you?"

Vardan's smile looked more feral than any man should. Zuleika thought she glimpsed something of a killer whale in his features. "We have several fishing villages, and each has its own watchtower, built of the limestone quarried at the northern end of the island. Most nights they only fish for the fruit of the sea. But sometimes, when the lookout spots a sail…my people turn to hunting instead. And their skill is unsurpassed in these waters, except by sharks."

Now Zuleika shivered at his chilling tone. "That still does not answer my question, your Highness," she said slowly. "How did you come to have the cargo of the *Rosa* in your cellar?"

He studied her for a long moment before he said, "That, I think you will need to see to believe, but such a battle is hardly a suitable place for a lady. Even such a fearless one as yourself. So I shall take you to the nearest village, and let my people tell you about the hunt. Perhaps you will believe them more than you believe me." Vardan turned on his heel and headed out of the cave the way they'd come, taking the torch and its light with him.

Zuleika considered using magic to light her way, but she dismissed the idea as quickly as it had come. Vardan distrusted witches, and if he found out who she was…he might be far less hospitable. So she hurried after him, back to daylight where the death-drenched darkness would be merely a memory.

Twenty-Seven

Lady Belle barely spoke a word during the ride to the village of Storhem. Even when he grew so sick of the silence that he began telling her the names of the farmers and their likely crop next season as they passed each field, she merely nodded, looking like her thoughts were far from him and the cursed isle.

Perhaps she had only feigned indifference to the slaughter Vardan had witnessed firsthand. Had she known one of the pirates, then? A brother, perhaps, or the father she kept mentioning?

No, Vardan decided. Her father could not have been a pirate. She'd been raised a lady, and no pirate he'd met was capable of so much as looking at a woman without planning to dishonour her before selling her into slavery. Lady Belle could not have been any man's slave.

Or had the pirate been her sweetheart, a man she waited for? Her father could not have known about him, or he would certainly have stopped the match, as any good father should. Allowing such scum to so much as look at Lady Belle, let alone touch her...

Something clawed at his insides, twisting and ripping in ways that made Vardan clench his hands into fists around Arion's reins. Jealousy, he realised. Because pirates were scum, but they were still men. Barely more than beasts, but still men. Unlike him.

What would it take to break the curse, so that a woman might look kindly upon him once more?

No. Down that road lay madness. Hope was a curse all its own, for it tasted as sweet as mead even as it dulled his senses.

Banishing hope was a simple matter.

"Have you a sweetheart?" Vardan asked. Ah, that had got her attention.

Lady Belle stared at him. "What did you say?"

"Do you have a sweetheart?" he repeated patiently. "A man you are betrothed to, or wish to be. Or someone your father has promised you to."

The lady bristled. "I am not cargo or a slave, to be bought and sold on a man's whim. I am of age, and both my hands and my heart are my own." As if to demonstrate, she tucked her cloak more closely around her so that it hid her hands. Her heart burned with pent-up fury – she could not hide the fire as it blazed out of her violet eyes.

For a wild moment, his own heart soared as he dared to hope again. But reality brought him back to earth abruptly. Vardan said, "Then I pity the man who has the courage to ask you for your hand, for your denial will undoubtedly drive him to despair. You are a rare woman, Lady Belle. Most women desire security, position, wealth or protection. Yet it seems to me you wish for none of these things. What desire drives you?"

She blinked, seemingly lost for words, but only for a moment. An impish grin lit her face. "Curiosity. First the fate of my father's ships and cargo, and now the nature of a powerful curse. I can't imagine being cursed and not doing everything in my power to break it. How have you not sought out a solution to your…affliction?"

Had she not listened to a word he'd said? "Of course I have. My brother – "

"Has it occurred to you that your brother might be lying, and that he knows less about curses than you do?" she interrupted, eyes flashing.

"Watch your words, Lady Belle. To speak ill of your

king is treason."

Instead of calming her, this seemed to only incense her further. "Thorn is not my king. He is a deceitful, dishonourable louse who had the astonishing good fortune to be the oldest son of a royal family to survive into adulthood. If he knows anything about curses, it is because he has somehow enslaved a witch. Even then, she would be a poor witch indeed if she told him everything." She paused for breath, looked into his eyes, and continued, "I am sorry if my words grieve you, for I know the king is your brother. Perhaps he was a good man once, or has become one since I was last at court."

She knew him. She'd met Thorn, and she knew him. Her impassioned words proved it. Perhaps a little too much passion, though, as if she was trying to convince him of her hatred for Thorn. Women didn't hate Thorn. They flocked to his bed. Did that mean she was some sort of spy for his brother?

"I love my brother," Vardan said. "And I am loyal to the king." There. Let her tell him that when she carried her report home to the capital.

"But what if he is wrong, and love is not the way to break the spell? Loyalty is not the same as blind obedience. Another witch as powerful as the one who cursed you might be able to lift the enchantment. I have…heard such things can happen." She bit her lip, as if she wanted to say more but didn't dare let the words out.

Vardan snorted. "In folktales and legends, perhaps. If my brother had wished to lie, or give me bad counsel, he would not have given me such an impossible task to break the spell. Either seduce a woman when none will even look at me, let alone love me, or kill a woman who does not deserve it. You are a woman, Lady Belle, so you tell me: could you love me?"

Those violet eyes turned on him, and he dropped his gaze so he wouldn't see the pity in them.

"I am not the sort of sheltered maiden who falls in love with the first man she meets. I scarcely know you, Vardan. I do not understand how you could lay under such a fearsome curse for five years and not seek help to lift it."

Now he lifted his head to meet her gaze. No woman had looked at him the way she did, as though he was not a beast. "For five years, I have been busy. Discharging my responsibilities as the Trade Master of this island. Fighting pirates, as you shall see. And in all those years…you are the first woman who can stand to look at me. For five years, I have had no hope of breaking the curse. Yet today…I begin to believe it might be possible. I ask you again: could you love me?"

Long did he look into her eyes, for he was loath to look away, even as a tear slipped down her cheek. Only then did Vardan feel the shame he should have felt earlier, in driving a woman to pain and tears. He was not usually so unchivalrous.

"I am sorry. I should not have asked such a personal question. Can you forgive me, Lady Belle?" he asked.

She nodded, and her silence returned. Somehow, this time it was worse.

Twenty-Eight

Zuleika cursed herself for opening her mouth. Vardan was loyal to his lying brother, and as long as he believed the king over her, he would never understand that it took much more than love to break a spell as powerful as the one on Beacon Isle. If he would only listen...

She'd been so caught up in the curse itself that she hadn't seen his question coming. One she did not know the answer to. Could she love him?

She was capable of love, for she loved her family. She had no husband or betrothed, so if she chose, she could give her hand and her heart to any man she wished. If by some miracle Vardan turned out to be the complete opposite of his brother, despite looking like him under the illusion, then perhaps, it was faintly possible that, if he were charming enough and she stayed for sufficient time, that she might...maybe...be capable of such a thing. Possibly.

But she had no right to raise his hopes, because she knew it didn't matter. Even if she loved him madly and married him, the curse would remain. And until she relieved him of his affliction, she had no right to his heart or his gratitude, and no business falling in love with anyone.

She bit her lip as Embarr carried her into the fishing village, whispering a spell under her breath that would allow her to see what the curse hid once more. She knew better than to look at Vardan, but she found she needed little reminding this time. As evening fell, the villagers had stopped work for the day, and they seemed to be preparing for some kind of festival.

"What is the date? Is a saint's day, or some other holy occasion that I have forgotten?" she asked.

The villagers, who looked very much like those at home, stopped to stare, but none seemed ready to volunteer an answer.

"Please, will someone tell me what you are celebrating?" she persisted, her gaze sweeping across the dozen or so people before her. People who were not used to being seen.

Finally, a man stepped forward. He ducked his head a few times before he ventured, "If it please you, m'lady, the prince gave the order that a feast should be prepared to celebrate his...your visit to Storhem. We have the best of today's catch, and he sent word from Harbourtown that the baker was to prepare special cakes to your ladyship's liking. Two tuns of wine were sent from the prince's cellars..."

Hastily, Zuleika cut him off by expressing her thanks. This seemed to satisfy the man, who hustled the others off to the village square.

Vardan reached her side.

Zuleika allowed herself a glance at him before turning her head away. "Still trying to seduce me with food and wine, I see."

She heard him sigh. "I am merely trying to entice you to stay," he said. "As you say, you've known me for less than a day. Perhaps if you remain on the island longer, you will get to know me better, and perhaps even consider..." She heard him swallow before he finished, "Helping all of these good citizens by lifting our curse."

Stung, she turned to meet his gaze squarely. "I will help. But..." Conscious of the villagers who might hear her, and not wanting to smash their hopes as she had his, she subsided. Unable to stare at his face any longer, she dismissed her spell. Better not to frighten the villagers by seeing them when no one else could.

"Thank you," was all he said. No more talk of love, to Zuleika's considerable relief.

Twenty-Nine

Vardan tried to keep still in his seat between Lady Belle and the village headman at the high table in the village hall, but his eyes kept darting to look at her. It didn't help that they sat so close he couldn't help jostling her. It would be so easy to reach around her, pull her to him and kiss her.

And make her hate him for the rest of his miserable life, he didn't doubt.

She behaved like a proper lady, of course. Her eyes surveyed the noisy hall, though there was little to see except food disappearing from trenchers. She didn't look the least bit alarmed by the invisible crowd, and she even conversed with the headman's wife, who sat beside her. What was the woman's name? He couldn't believe he'd forgotten. He knew everyone on Beacon Isle.

Lady Belle's musical laughter stole his attention entirely. "Prince Vardan, is it true what Birgitte tells me? That when you were a boy, you once stole a fishing boat and led the other fishermen a merry chase around the whole island before they caught up to you?"

He'd forgotten that. "Yes," he said grudgingly, "but they did not catch up to me until I let them do so. I had a wager with my brother that I could singlehandedly sail around the island. There was a pretty maid we both liked and the winner of the wager would get a kiss, she said. So I rode up to Storhem, borrowed a fishing boat and set off. I sailed around the island, sure enough, and brought the little boat into Harbourtown, as proud as a prince could be. Then I gave the boat back to her owners. Not a scratch on her, I swear."

Lady Belle's voice dropped low so that only he could hear it over the hubbub in the hall. "What did your brother say when you won the wager? Was the maid's kiss worth all that effort?"

Vardan swallowed. This was the part he had never told a soul. "I do not know. When I arrived at the house, neither the maid nor my brother were anywhere to be found." Not by those who didn't know Thorn well, at least. For his brother...Vardan had found them doing much more than kissing. No, he did not want to remember that day, and he did not think it fit for a maiden's ears, either. Better for her to believe in chivalry and love and not all that animal grunting in the hayloft as two sweaty, naked bodies rutted like...well, beasts. Or that the girl had died trying to birth what Vardan assumed had been Thorn's bastard less than a year later. "How do you like the fish?" he asked.

"Delicious," she replied. "I have never eaten fish cooked with saffron before. It is far too rare a spice to use where I come from, and yet here, I see the whole village eating more saffron in this one meal than I have eaten in my lifetime before today."

Vardan frowned. "What do you expect? As you said earlier today, the purpose of trade goods is to be sold, not stockpiled, and when the goods are food...they must be eaten, or they spoil. Once the curse is lifted, we will be able to share the fruits of our saffron crops with the rest of the country, but while Beacon Isle is enchanted...we must use what we have. After all, without trade, we must grow all our own food. That includes spices."

Lady Belle stared at him. "Saffron is grown here?"

Hadn't he told her as much as they passed the

134

crocus fields? "Of course. We rode past the fields on the way here."

It was her turn to frown. "I must have been so deep in thought about your curse that I did not notice. When we pass by there again, please remind me what I missed."

"Better to think about flowers than curses, Lady Belle. Thinking about this curse will not cure it, or someone would have lifted it already. Enough talk about curses for tonight. For cursed or no, this is a celebration feast and no feast is complete without dancing!" He roared the last word so that the whole hall would hear him.

Tables and benches scraped as many hands pulled them to the side of the hall.

"Dancing? Is that wise?" Lady Belle asked.

"Wise? Perhaps not. But enjoyable, certainly. I have never met a woman who did not dearly like to dance. Will you be the exception to that, too, Lady Belle?" Vardan prayed that he hadn't made a mistake. All the ladies at court loved dancing, and he remembered the rowdier village dances here when he was a boy.

"I own I enjoy dancing as much as my sisters, or any woman alive, but I meant is it wise to dance in a room full of people when most of them are invisible? I might not know the steps if the dances are different to those at home. What if I were to tread on someone's foot, or bump into them?"

Vardan laughed. "A lady as graceful as you would never do such a thing, I am certain."

"But, your Highness – "

The wooden door to the hall crashed open and a man stood silhouetted in the open doorway. Breathlessly, he announced, "Ship sighted to the south. Two pirate vessels, closing fast."

Of all the nights...Vardan cursed inwardly. There would be no dancing tonight. "Get her to safety," he called over his shoulder as he strode out of the hall. He should have checked the mirror this morning, as was his usual habit, to see if any merchant or pirate ships were nearby. He'd been so distracted by the woman that he'd forgotten, and the crew of this new ship might pay the price for his carelessness. The war against piracy was far more important than breaking some silly curse. Most days he remembered that, but today he'd been selfish. And now...

"Where are you going?" Lady Belle demanded from right behind him.

"Into battle, which is no place for a woman," he replied.

"You also said it was a battle I must see to believe," she returned. Vardan wasn't sure how her eyes managed to flash in the darkness, yet they did.

"The aftermath, yes, but not from the middle of the

fighting. We lose men and boats all the time when we hunt pirates. They know they have nothing to lose and for all our advantages, some of our men still die in the skirmish. If anything were to happen to you…if you were hurt, thrown into the water, drowned, killed…Lady Belle, you do not know what you are asking."

"I am not defenceless, you know," she said.

Vardan sighed. "But you are visible."

"So are you."

"Which is why I will not be part of a hunting party," Vardan explained patiently. "I climb the watchtower and command the fleet while the ghost boats surround the ships. They dispatch the pirates, bring the cargo to shore, and any crew who remain take the ship's boats to safety. We have tried offering them sanctuary at Beacon Isle, but word has spread that the island is haunted, and no superstitious sailor wants to land here any more."

"How can you possibly command ships so far out on the ocean?" Lady Belle demanded. "You cannot see them so far away. They cannot see you in the dark, and they could not hear you over the sounds of battle."

"We have a code of sorts," Vardan began, then stopped. Was that why she was here? To learn the codes so that she could share them with pirates? Surely not. Or was it the magic mirror she was after? That would be a prize indeed, if she knew about it. If she did not, he would not be the one to tell her. Let her believe the code was their only means of communication. "It is of my own invention," he added with considerable pride.

"And what do the village women do?"

"They keep house, clear away the remains of the feast, put the children to bed, and see that when the menfolk return from a hard night's work, there is breakfast waiting for them in the morning," Vardan said. As good wives should, he thought but didn't say.

"I will stand watch with you," she announced.

He cursed. "No, woman, you will not." Without another word, he kicked Arion into a gallop, sure she would not follow.

Thirty

Stubborn fool, Zuleika thought as she mounted Embarr. Did he honestly think she would allow farmers and fishermen to die in a battle she could end with a single spell? Or that she wouldn't do everything in her power to save the crew of the ship the pirates were attacking?

She cast a spell to guide her to him, and was surprised to find Arion only a few hundred yards from the village, tied up outside the clifftop watchtower. Zuleika left Embarr beside her stablemate and set off up the stairs to the top of the tower, where loud swearing had erupted from several throats, including Vardan's.

"Do we have enough people to take both ships? That pincer move is new. I want them all executed before they can pass word about that particular tactic on to their fellows."

"We're not sure, master," said a second voice. "We've never tried to take on two ships at the same time before."

Zuleika peered out of one of the tower windows as she climbed. The three ships were surprisingly easy to see, lit up by some peculiar kind of fire that floated on the water without extinguishing.

Magic. It had to be. First Thorn, now pirates. Would all the scum of the earth enslave witches? This would not be borne.

Already simmering with anger, Zuleika now blazed with fury. She bit down so hard on her lip that it hurt, but she barely noticed the sting. "Pirate scum, show your true form," she murmured. "Never to be men again until you repent your wicked life and vow never to return to piracy." The spell shot out in a bolt of violet fire, splitting into two as it homed in on the pirate ships.

She both felt and saw the spell take effect, bursting into clouds of purple sparks on the decks of all three ships. Only then did she see the fishing fleet close in around the vessels, looking eerily empty in the floating firelight.

Whispering a second spell, she sent it out across the waves to search for the witch, but the spell circled the ships without settling on anyone. If there was no spellcaster aboard the ships, how on earth could water burn so?

She hurried up to Vardan. Perhaps he could answer her question. "Send word to Sillhem to ready their boats," she heard him say. "Have the men of Raggarn ready to receive the cargo. And the women...ask them to pray and prepare for the wounded. This will not be an easy fight."

As she entered the room, two men swept past her, heading down the steps to carry out Vardan's orders. Vardan was too busy peering out the window to notice her, so she took a deep breath and cast her mind toward the ships. There was no fighting, merely the salvaging of cargo before the merchant ship sank. One of the pirate ships had rammed it, and water already gushed through the splintered bow.

So that was the *Rosa*'s fate. Impaled by a pirate ship. Had the *Rosa*'s demise been lit by the same strange candles dotting the sea surface now?

"How goes the battle?" she asked.

Vardan glanced back at her and swore under his breath. "I told you to stay in the village where it is safe, not follow me." In this light, he looked like an eagle now, with beakish nose and bright, searching eyes.

Zuleika took a step closer to him. "It seems safe enough here. No pirates, and the ships are so far away. I did not realise you could see so clearly from here, even at night."

He stared at her for a long moment before he said, "That's Greek fire. A strange substance that burns even in water. I've seen it cling to a man's clothes and burn him alive, no matter how many buckets of water we threw at him. Among men of honour, it is considered too terrible a weapon to use on an enemy, but pirates have no honour and will resort to such tactics to win. Battle is not pretty, Lady Belle, and one with pirates is uglier still."

So it wasn't magic at all. No wonder she had not found a witch. "I have seen it before. Naphtha, they called it. Water is the wrong element to combat it with. What you need is earth. You must smother it with dust."

"Better to smother the pirates who know how to make it, so that they cannot use it again," he said grimly. Now, he surely looked like a shark, the cold, predatory fish that killed without conscience. What kind of curse transformed his face from moment to moment? As if it did not simply turn him into a beast, but the beast that best reflected his thoughts at any given time. "The only good pirate is a dead one."

Zuleika agreed with the sentiment, but still she said,

"There are not many men who know how to make Greek fire, as you call it. The secret was known to a djinn who was enslaved to a lamp in punishment for sharing the secret of its fabrication with his king's enemies." A particularly pesky djinn she knew to be safe in the same enchanted cave where she'd imprisoned him. "More likely, they stole a cargo that contained some of the stuff."

"Perhaps," Vardan said, his gaze returning to the ships. "We shall see what my people bring ashore." He pointed at the fleet of boats clustered around the three ships. As if on command, one peeled away from the cluster and headed for shore.

Finally, Zuleika understood. "You man the watchtowers, watching for pirates or ships in trouble. Then, you send out your ghost fleet to do battle with the pirates. Once they have defeated the pirates, they bring the cargo from the stricken ship ashore. Are all the ships sunk?"

"Not all. Sometimes, when we have enough warning, we can save the merchant ship and it continues on its way. But word has spread about the ghost fleet, so savvy pirates flee when they see us. Yet a pirate who flees is not defeated, so we remain vigilant, for we know they will return, as they did today. They may lack honour, but they are still men who learn from their mistakes."

Zuleika opened her mouth to tell him that the only men aboard the ships were his own people and the merchant ship's crew, but that would mean confessing to casting the spell that transformed the pirates. Sighing, she closed her mouth again.

Vardan continued, "There is little to see here now. If the boats are carrying cargo, the battle is won. They will work through the night to save what is aboard the ship before she sinks. You should get some sleep, Lady Belle. Ask the headwoman, Birgitte, to find you a bed here, or you can return to my house, if you do not mind the ride."

Yes, sleep sounded quite tempting around now. Spellcasting, especially multiple transformations, was tiring at the best of times, let alone at the end of a long day's ride and feasting.

"Then I shall bid you good night, your Highness, and thank you for a delightful day," she said. She made it partway down the stairs before she heard his response.

"The pleasure is all mine, Lady Belle," he said so softly she suspected he hadn't intended her to hear it at all.

The prince was a strange man to enjoy arguing with her all day. Grinning broadly, Zuleika descended.

Thirty-One

It was almost dawn by the time Zuleika reached the prince's home, but falling into bed was certainly worth the ride. She fell asleep almost instantly, safe in the knowledge that Inga and the other servants would guard her chamber until she awoke.

She slept late into the day, waking only when she heard Inga's voice calling her name. Well, not her name…the one the prince had given her.

"My lady, you must dress for the feast," Inga said.

No, the feast was last night. A noisy affair in the village hall where they served yellow fish, smothered in saffron. And then there'd been pirates…

"My lady, the prince insists that you must sit by his

side at the feast. There is always a big celebration after a victory at sea and this one is a double victory, he says, with no men lost. The people are saying it is a miracle, which must be your doing. A lady who can perform miracles can surely lift the curse, is what they say in town. They all wish to see the prince's lady, and you must look the part."

Wonderful. Having hundreds of invisible people staring at her, filled with such hope, when she was still no closer to breaking the spell. She'd never found a curse she couldn't counter until now. How this one could elude her so...

"If you do not rise on your own, I shall tell the master. He will drag you from your bed," Inga announced.

Vardan in her bed? No. Oh, no. His brother had been bad enough.

"My head hurts," Zuleika said, sitting up. "I hope you have willow bark tea."

"'Tis cold, but it should still work," Inga replied, gesturing at the tray beside the bed.

Zuleika gulped down the tea, then tore into the saffron cake sitting beside it. It, too, was cold, but still as delicious as the ones she'd devoured yesterday.

Behind her, the door opened. "I have the dress, my lady," said Greta, breathless with what sounded like excitement.

"Show her," commanded Inga.

Fabric rustled as Greta laid the gown on the chest at the end of the bed, and Zuleika gasped. The dress was made of yellow silk, bright as the sun. She couldn't stop herself from reaching out to touch it, to see if it was truly real.

"It's beautiful," Zuleika breathed.

"It was aboard one of the pirate ships, my lady, in a chest with no merchant's markings. The master's steward said it looked like a queen's dowry, for the gowns are all new, but there was no woman aboard any of the ships."

Perhaps the pirates had killed her, or she had sent her dowry ahead of her marriage, Zuleika told herself, forcing her hand to leave the silk alone. "I am not a queen. It is too rich a gown for me."

"Half the villagers out there are ready to declare you the Blessed Virgin, Queen of Heaven, come to save them," Inga said grimly. "You have already worn the Dowager Queen's gowns, and this belongs to no one now. If not you, then who will wear it?"

"I suppose…" Zuleika began.

"In this gown, you shall light up the room. The master will not be able to take his eyes off you, I promise." Inga swallowed. "If only for one night, my lady, in the hope that you can break this curse…please, would you wear it?"

147

Once again, Zuleika could not refuse the woman's earnest plea. And wearing the beautiful silk gown was hardly a hardship.

"I will," she declared. If only wearing the beautiful dress would be enough to break the spell, but Zuleika knew it would take far more than that.

Thirty-Two

This was a terrible idea, Vardan told himself as he took his place at the high table in his own hall. He'd spent all night overseeing the salvage operation, though it had not been necessary, because he knew without a doubt his dreams would be filled with her when he slept.

He had snatched a few hours' sleep in the afternoon, which had left him feeling more tired than ever as the maiden with the violet eyes had danced just out of his reach, laughing at him. He was afraid to look into Lady Belle's eyes today.

A woman who could discuss war, or at least the weapons used in one, and took pride in victory. A girl who understood shipping and commerce as well as most merchants. A lady who saw his brother for what he was. A remarkable beauty who arrived mysteriously by magical means who yet wished to help free him of his enchantment. Could a man find himself in love with a woman he had known for only a few days? Never had he experienced such desire for a woman. More than beauty, more than brilliance...some sort of magic drew him to her. Lady Belle, the lady who would never give him her hand or her heart, for she did not even trust him with her name.

He wanted to pound the table into splinters with his fist, destroying everything in the hall like the rabid beast he resembled until he quelled his frustration. He might tear the house down before that happened.

Benches scraped and pushed back from tables as the room fell silent.

Lady Belle, haloed by the afternoon sun streaking through the window, looking like an avenging angel in glowing gold. He had no doubt that she was the one who could break the spell. He wanted to fall to his knees in worship.

But that would not do.

Instead, Vardan leaped to his feet, realising that his people were more courteous than he, for they had already moved to stand for the lady.

Her knowing smile seemed to see straight into his

heart as she looked right at him for just a moment before her gaze swept the room.

Rolf cleared his throat. In his best sonorous voice, he announced, "The Lady Belle, our guest of honour."

Jealousy blazed through Vardan's body as she turned that smile on his steward before her eyes returned to Vardan.

"The honour is mine, receiving your hospitality as a guest in this hall," she responded in ringing tones. The tones of a lady used to speaking in court, so that she might be heard above the sly whisperings of the other courtiers. She followed this statement with a deep curtsey, spreading her silk skirt so it caught the light even more. Magnificent.

Vardan stumbled forward, feeling every eye upon him as he bowed and offered her his arm for the interminable walk back to the high table. Her hand rested on his arm so lightly it should have felt like no weight at all, but Vardan felt the urge to drop to his knees at every step. How could one woman hold so much power over him? It was almost as if she had cast a spell on him.

If only the curse could be broken by him falling in love instead of her. For his heart, his soul…he had lost all of them to Lady Belle.

Thirty-Three

Exhaustion seemed to slow the prince's steps as he escorted her to the high table. Zuleika said nothing as she matched his pace, keeping a happy smile on her face for all the onlookers she could hear but not see. The temptation to cast a quick spell so that she could see them all was almost irresistible, but removing the illusion that hid the prince's people would also reveal his true face, instead of the one he wore now.

Invisible servants helped her into her chair and pushed it closer to the table, as others did the same for Vardan. Tonight, they sat alone at the high table, but still close enough to touch. Close enough for conversation, Zuleika corrected herself, which would not be heard by the rest of the hall, who had begun talking amongst themselves again.

"Were there many injuries sustained in last night's battle?" she enquired as she selected some meat from the platter before her.

"None that I know of," Vardan replied. "My men are calling it a bloodless victory, for not even a drop of pirate blood was shed, or so they say. If they did not all tell the same tale, I would doubt it, but fifty huntsmen cannot be wrong. Pirates do not bleed green unless there is sorcery at work."

"If no blood was shed, how can anyone know it was green?" Zuleika asked.

Vardan shrugged. "One moment they saw pirates swarming the *Trinity*, and the next…they were gone, leaving nothing but some green scum on the deck where they had once stood. Only magic can do that, which means there must have been a witch on the *Trinity*. She was so close…and yet I let her get away. You are my only hope now, Lady Belle."

She longed to tell him the truth – that the only witch present last night was her, but he would never say her true name the way his voice caressed that silly nickname. He would spit curses, order his men to seize her and send her to his brother.

She would not let that happen.

Zuleika sipped from her goblet. The warm, spiced

153

mead soothed her, reminding her of home, so she drank more.

"Will you give me hope, Lady Belle?"

Her breath caught in her throat at the prince's beseeching tone, barely a whisper away from outright begging. "There is hope, your Highness. All curses can be broken. The only question is...at what price?" she said.

He spread his hands wide. "What can I offer you that will make you love me? The deepest desire of your heart – if I can give it to you, it is yours."

"Love is not enough to break the spell," she said. "Even if I were to..." Those eyes! So much feeling, it was enough to rock her to her very soul. No woman could look into those eyes and be unmoved. Zuleika swallowed and managed to continue, "If I were to give you my heart, it would not be enough. It took magic to cast the spell, and only magic can break it."

"You have enchanted me, Lady Belle. I know no more powerful spell than the one you have cast over me since you arrived at Beacon Isle. You light up the whole island, though the evil enchantress cursed us with darkness." He seized her hand in his. "Please say you will stay."

He would not ask her that if he knew she was an enchantress, Zuleika was certain.

He released her. "I realise I have little to offer you

until the curse is lifted, but if you could find it in your heart to help, and perhaps wait a little, I will send my men after the witch. Together, I am sure you can find a solution to this…affliction."

A floating serving platter, borne by an invisible manservant, cut their conversation short, to Zuleika's relief, as she concentrated on selecting something suitable from the selection before her. She had eaten almost nothing all day, and she was famished.

Fortunately, Vardan had a similar appetite, so they ate in silence for a little while, before someone brought more mead to fill her cup.

Instead of resuming their conversation, Vardan rose to give a toast. "To yet another pirate victory, and the health of our beautiful guest."

The hall erupted in cheering as everyone raised their cups and drank. The prince's pledge was the first of many, it seemed, as the other men in the hall took the opportunity to toast the health, good fortune and future of Zuleika and the prince, as well as that of their own people.

Just as Zuleika worried she'd run out of mead, someone blew a particularly loud blast on a horn. A group of musicians she'd neither seen nor heard until now drew her attention to the alcove at the side of the hall. In truth, she still could not see them, but their instruments were visible, and the sounds they made as they tuned their instruments were certainly audible.

At least, it was until people started pushing the tables to the sides of the hall, making enough noise to drown out even the most determined horn blower.

"Would you like to dance, Lady Belle?" Vardan asked, rising from his seat only to bow before her.

Rowdy cheers urged him on.

She opened her mouth to repeat last night's protests.

"Since the curse, we only dance caroles in a chain. You needn't worry about the steps. Simply hold onto those before and behind you, and follow where they lead." He held out his hand. "I will not lead you astray, Lady Belle. You have my word."

This time, she believed him. He was no pirate, or her spell would have turned him into green scum the previous night. Vardan and his people did not deserve the terrible curse Thorn and his pet witch had visited on them.

She took a deep breath. "And I will do everything within my power to free you from this curse. I give you my word, your Highness."

He grinned. "Then let's dance!" He seized her hand, pulling her from the dais and into the crowd below.

Thirty-Four

The warmth of her hand in his sent Vardan's heart racing like never before. No one touched him willingly, but this was so much more. She'd given him her hand. It might only be for a dance now, but he vowed it would be more if he could persuade her to accept him. Once the curse was lifted…

The music changed, signifying that it was time to break the chain they had woven around the room and form up into couples. Without thinking, he placed his hands at her waist and lifted her, spinning around like everyone else in time to the music.

Her laughter swirled around him, the most joyous sound he'd ever heard. Her hands landed on his shoulders, perhaps to steady herself, but he would never drop her. Instead, he set her gently on her feet, and led her through the steps of the couples' dance. Though her brow creased occasionally when she made a misstep, her delighted smile never left her face. Heaven, this was surely heaven.

Yet the song ended and Vardan bowed to his partner. She dipped a curtsey, keeping her laughing eyes level with his.

His voice was hoarse in his throat. "Another dance, Lady Belle?"

The room fell silent, so her breathless answer rang out through the hall, "Oh yes."

The musicians struck up a country dance tune, a lovers' dance that played almost nonstop on the May Day festival, when the winter ended. It should have sounded strange with the island still shrouded in snow, but tonight it was perfect.

Whispers spread like wind through the hall as people shuffled toward the walls, leaving space for the dancers. For the master and the lady he wished was his, Vardan realised.

In a room full of invisible people, he and Lady Belle danced alone. Her skirts flared out as she spun with the steps, before whirling back into his embrace. Every time he released her, his heart died a little, until she returned to him a moment later as the dance brought them back together.

He heard the village women sigh each time, echoing the burst of feeling in his own heart. Country dances were for peasants, not royalty or nobility, but right now he didn't care. The stateliest court dances were dull compared to the sparkle that lit her eyes as she danced in his arms. If the members of the court were ever to dance with such abandon, they would never agree to arranged marriages with people they'd never met.

Vardan would never agree to any woman but Belle after this night. Every moment she spent in his arms, he wanted to extend into forever. Could she...would she ever be his?

The song ended far too soon, and Lady Belle drew him toward where servants stood with trays of drinks.

"I have a thirst that must be quenched, your Highness. I have never danced quite so...energetically before. When my sisters spoke of court dances, they always sounded so...sedate. Not something I wished to take part in. Yet this...this...I feel like I could dance all night, though I shall quite wear out my slippers." A silk-clad foot peeped out from under her skirt, and she clutched at his shoulder to keep her balance.

She might have clutched at his heart, the touch jolted him so much. Vardan covered her hand with his.

159

"With you, I, too, could dance all night, and all day, too. But the curse…"

Her eyes seemed to glow with violet fire once more. "I will find a way. There must be something in my mother's library. If – "

Her mother's library was nothing compared to the collection here, most of it illuminated in the monastery's own scriptorium. And this library held something far more valuable than books. "I have a better idea," Vardan interrupted. "Come with me."

This time when he took her hand, it felt like the most natural thing in the world.

"Won't the others notice?" she asked, glancing back. Another song played and from the sound of feet on stone, Vardan guessed that the dancers had returned to the floor.

"Perhaps, but this is not court. We don't stand on ceremony here. This is a feast to celebrate a victory – a victory they won, not I. We shall return before they have finished this dance."

"All right."

She allowed him to lead her out of the hall and into the part of the house that used to be a monastery. He bypassed the monks' cells without a second glance, but Lady Belle slowed.

"Are these…prison cells?" she asked.

Vardan laughed. "No, the monks slept here when it

was a monastery. They are sleeping cells, much like in a convent, I imagine. None are held here against their will. Their faith compels them, or so the brothers say. I used to sleep in one when I was studying with them as a boy. For all that they have no fire, they are still warm, for they are above the scriptorium. A fire burns there year round to help preserve the books. I will show you."

"You are taking me to your library," Belle said slowly, her smile dawning once more. "I should like to see that."

"Then come." He tugged at her hand, and she came willingly, her steps quickening to match his. Ah, a lady who liked books. If Vardan wasn't in love with her already, he wold have fallen a second time. She was perfection itself.

He threw the doors open and led her inside. Candles lit the room, as always, but Belle's gratifying gasp as she surveyed a library that rivalled the great hall for size made him examine it anew. Even the king did not have so many books in his palace in the capital.

"It would take a lifetime to read them all," she breathed, reaching for the nearest shelf but stopping before she touched anything.

Vardan grinned. "A few years, yes, but not a lifetime. I know from experience." He coughed. "If you wish it, you may stay here as long as it takes you to read them all. A lifetime, if that is your wish." Oh, how he longed to kiss her. The way she looked at him now, as if he was a man and not a beast. First, they must break the curse. "But I have something I must show you."

He drew her to the window, where a chest held his most prized possession. He drew out the well-wrapped bundle, then paused with the heavy thing in his hands. "This is a magical object, but it will not hurt you," he promised. "You need only look at it, if you wish. I will not ask you to touch it if you don't wish to."

Vardan expected to see fear in her eyes, but Lady Belle merely nodded as she turned expectant eyes on the bundle.

He folded back the cloth, revealing a mirror as shiny as the day when Sir Ryder had first handed it to him. Before the curse. Now, it was his only view to a world he could never be a part of.

"Have you ever seen its like?" Vardan murmured.

To his surprise, Belle nodded. "My mother owned just such a looking glass. She kept it in her library, too."

"This is no ordinary looking glass, for it shows far more than the beauty of its owner. It was a gift from my brother on my name day. I check it every morning and every night for pirates and approaching ships, so that my people might be prepared for the hunt. It shows more than ships, though. This glass can show you whatever you desire, wherever it might be in the world." Vardan grinned at her surprise. "So you see, it is nothing like your mother's mirror. I only have to fog it with my breath, like so –" he breathed on the glass "– and focus on what I desire to see. Once the fog clears, the mirror reveals what I ask." Vardan moistened his lips. "What I long for most right now is to find a witch who can break the curse, as she slayed the pirates. If I am not wrong, it will show the crew of the *Trinity* in their boat, and among them...the witch." He held the mirror up so Zuleika could see. "What do you see, Lady Belle?"

Thirty-Five

Zuleika's own reflection looked back. Nothing more. She sighed. "I only see myself, your Highness. There is nothing magical about your looking glass."

Vardan frowned. "That isn't possible." He breathed on the glass again. "Show me the crew of the *Trinity*," he commanded. "There! See?"

Zuleika inspected the mirror again. This time, the prince was right. The mirror showed a tiny boat, dwarfed by dark, wintry waves as the men huddled together for warmth. And there it was. Men, without a witch or woman among them. "I see the boat, but no witch."

Without warning, the prince's head was beside hers,

so close their cheeks touched. "I believe you are right. Then where is she?"

Zuleika swallowed. I am here, she wanted to say, but she didn't want to spoil such a perfect evening. If anything, she wanted to return with him to the great hall, so that he might hold her in his arms while they danced the night away. Was it so wrong to want one more night?

He cupped her cheek, shifting so he could look into her eyes. "Lady Belle…"

She squeezed her eyes shut. If she stared into his soul any longer, she would be lost. "That is not my name." She wanted to tell him, if only to hear his say her name with the same adoration as he used for her nickname, but that would never happen. Her name on his lips. His lips…

"Then tell me," he whispered.

Zuleika seized his head in her hands and kissed him. Clumsily at first, for she had never kissed a man before, but then Vardan recovered from his surprise and kissed her back. Just as in the dance in the great hall, she followed his lead, until she was so breathless she had to stop.

"Lady…"

Zuleika shook her head. "My mother once told me to beware the man who could steal my breath with a kiss, for he would steal my heart, too, and I would be lost."

"You are not lost here. I have you, and this will be your home, if you wish it." Vardan's arms tightened around her. "It doesn't matter what your name is. Not to me. If you do not wish to tell me, you will be Lady Belle for as long as I live."

Madness had seized her. She could become Lady Belle in truth, as the prince kissed her breathless. "Yes," she murmured, lifting her lips for another kiss.

Another, and another, as their tongues twined in a couples' dance that was far more intimate than their last. Breathless, yet gasping, lost and also unmistakably found in the prince's arms, feeling none of winter's chill as his love warmed her from the inside in places she had never felt heat before. She kissed him harder, growing bolder as her hands slid over his shoulders to feel hard muscle under his tunic. "Oh, Vardan," she sighed, cuddling against his chest.

"So you will stay, my fearless lady?" he asked.

Zuleika lifted her gaze to his face. Her answer died on her lips as her eyes widened in horror. A scream ripped out of her throat as she tore away from him and ran.

Thirty-Six

Her lips were sweeter than spiced mead as she kissed him, and Vardan knew this was no dream. For a moment, he dared to let his mind wander from kissing her to wedding her to bedding her…

Then she looked at him and it all went to hell.

Her scream still rang in his ears, freezing him in place as she bolted. Vardan let her go, for he knew what she'd seen. The beast, not the man. Yet she'd still kissed him, fangs and all, so that for one blessed moment, he'd believed…

In an unattainable dream. No one could love a beast.

On the other side of his house, the merriment

continued, but in the privacy of the library, invisible at last, the master wept.

Thirty-Seven

Eyes open or closed, Zuleika couldn't help but see his face. Vardan's face, exactly like his brother's. She hadn't cast a spell, drawn blood, broken the curse…none of it, and yet the illusion had shown him as the most beastly creature of all: the king.

"My lady!"

Zuleika heard Greta's voice, but didn't see the maid, and still she ran.

What kind of curse turned a man into a beast one moment, and a human monster the next?

One she could not break. Because if she did…the man she loved would look like the man she hated most. No matter how hideous he looked while cursed, she could still bear to look upon his face. But to look at Vardan and see Thorn…

No. That was why she must go.

Zuleika bit her lip, whispering a spell of invisibility to cloak her own form. Now she was just another reveller as she returned to the great hall, unknown and unseen. The doors were open and the gates, too, for men who had drunk too much to remember or even see a chamber pot were relieving themselves in the snow.

Ah, men were the same everywhere. Pissing contests would always occur as long as men had their manhoods.

Would Vardan boast to his brother that he had kissed the girl, only for Thorn to laugh and say he'd bedded her before she'd even met Vardan? Well, she'd curse them both for it. Thorn with childlessness, and Vardan by not removing his existing curse. She could do it, she was certain, if she understood the nature of it. But she would not.

Instead, she would leave.

Zuleika marched out the gate, wishing she had thought to bring a cloak against the biting cold. No matter. She would not be outside for long. Snow had not fallen today, so the road was clear, though the drifts lay deep on either side. She touched a finger to her bitten lip, pausing only long enough to see it stained red with blood, before she traced a portal in the air. A portal home.

Her hand arched up, then descended, letting the single drop of blood touch the cleared ground. The portal glowed purple-white before the enchantress stepped through and both vanished from Beacon Isle.

Thirty-Eight

What kind of curse turned a man into a beast one moment, and a human monster the next? A week Zuleika had been home, since her father welcomed both her and the news that his merchandise was safe, if inaccessible under the watchful eyes of the master of Beacon Isle, yet it was Vardan who had occupied her thoughts every waking moment, and some of her dreams, too.

She resisted the thought for a week before she finally capitulated and ventured into her mother's bower. Hers now.

Instead of pulling out books at random, Zuleika sat in the middle of the room, as she had been taught to do, and breathed deeply for focus. When she felt she had achieved this, she cast a spell for wisdom and asked for the knowledge she needed to break the spell, something she should have done long ago.

An enchantress was gifted shortly after her birth by a more senior enchantress with all the collective knowledge she would need to master her craft. Millennia of experience, passed down through countless generations, the wisdom of the ages. She could ask for answers and receive them from the vast repository of knowledge, mixed with her own memories, but it required focus. And the right questions.

What kind of curse turned a man into a monster?

A curse that revealed the darkest, most beastly aspects of his nature, her memories whispered. So that they will become visible to all those who look at him.

What kind of curse transformed not just a man, but his lands as well?

A curse that forbids his lands from offering welcome to anyone who approaches them.

What manner of curse could turn the population of an entire island invisible?

A curse that makes all those loyal to a man disappear, when he is the island's beloved leader.

Who would sentence a man to suffer such a curse?

No one. No one would willingly doom any man to

such a fate.

Then how did Vardan come to be cursed?

The mirror. Her mother's mirror. Not one like it – the mirror itself. Far-seeing, irresistible…and cursed. Twice. By Zuleika's own hand.

How did he come to possess it?

He is the king's brother. The king made him a gift of the mirror.

Why?

Because the king sees him as an enemy. He sees everyone more powerful than he as an enemy. He is a treacherous snake who deserves his fate.

But Prince Vardan does not.

No. The prince deserves to be loved and to have the curse lifted. His people deserve to see their loyalty rewarded by the breaking of their curse.

Is it true, then, that love can break the spell?

Only if it was cast with love, or a loophole allowing love to break it. If there is no loophole, then only two people can break the spell. Either a caster more powerful than the one who cast the curse; or the caster herself. But the price will be high, especially when the spell is recast by a cursed item so many times. Better to build a loophole when a spell is first cast.

Zuleika's mouth grew dry, though she hadn't spoken a single word aloud.

And what if there is no single caster more powerful

than the original one?

Then it will take a group of casters to use their collective power to remove the spell, but if that happens, they will see the damage this curse has wrought, and once the curse is undone, they will come after the caster. Enslave her like the djinn, for such wickedness will not be tolerated.

They would enslave her to the mirror, wouldn't they? So every day she could look upon the man she loved, knowing she had caused his suffering and that of all his people, when she could have prevented it, and see the hatred in his eyes.

Better to die than live as a slave.

Vardan and his people deserved to be free. No matter what the cost.

Thirty-Nine

Show me the girl. Show me Lady Belle. Show her to me.

The words echoed in Vardan's head all day and all night, tempting him to peer into the mirror to see her again, but he resisted. Why would he want to see the woman who was no different to anyone else? She couldn't stand the sight of him. So much so that she'd disappeared from the island not long after he'd made the mistake of kissing her.

Some of the villagers had admitted to seeing a flash of purple lightning that night, just as he had on the night of her arrival. Perhaps Thorn's witch had summoned Belle back against her will, but Vardan doubted it. The girl had run for a reason. And though he knew little of the lady, Vardan was certain Belle was no pawn in this game. Whoever she was.

Thorn's new queen, perhaps?

Jealousy burned him again at that thought, but there was little he could do to combat it. He wanted her in his arms, not his brother's, but if the lady did not want him...he would not waste his time pining after her, nor shed another tear. His moment of weakness had passed; he must be strong for his people, and continue to hunt pirates.

That's what he needed the mirror for. If he checked hourly instead of daily, what was the harm?

He breathed on the mirror, wishing to see the nearest pirate vessel, and the mirror flared with violet light as the image formed. Violet, just like Lady Belle's strange lightning. And her eyes. He'd never forget her eyes. Eyes that looked at him with what he'd thought was love, if only for a moment.

Vardan peered at the ship, trying to judge its location and how far it was from the island.

He did not feel the curse settling another layer of the spell over him and the rest of the island, as it had done every time he'd used the magic mirror. He had done this more than a thousand times – what was once more?

Forty

Zuleika opened a portal into the prince's library, hoping everyone would be asleep and not see her arrival. Sure enough, the room was empty, though the candles still burned. She knew what she had to do. Better to die than live as a slave, she reminded herself.

The chest was still there, and inside it was the bundle that contained the mirror. She unwrapped it carefully. Tears stung her eyes as she glimpsed the jewelled rose on the back, for it had been so long since she'd last seen it.

Zuleika lifted her mother's beautiful mirror, not daring to peer into it for fear she'd curse herself into revealing the frightened mouse she felt like right now.

She wanted to know where Vardan was, so that she might see him one last time, but she also dreaded meeting him. If she did, she would have to confess everything, for he deserved to know the truth, and she couldn't bear to lie to him any longer, even if he would hate her, knowing what she'd done.

She balled her free hand into a fist, smashing it into the mirror. The glass shattered, sending shards into her hand and wrist. Blood trickled, beaded, then spurted as she pulled out the pieces. All the while, she held her bleeding hand over the broken mirror, telling it to break the curse, break the curse, break the curse, for every time it had been cast. Vardan might have looked into the mirror a hundred, a thousand, or ten thousand times in the years it had remained in his possession, and if it took a drop of blood to dispel each time it had cursed him, she might drain her body of blood and it would not be enough. But still she let it flow, pooling on the frame and the few fragments of silvered glass that remained. This was her fault, and only she could free the island of its enchantment. If it took her lifeblood, then so be it. She should have known better than to cast such a curse in the first place. If she lived, she would never curse another object again.

Zuleika fell to her knees, then slowly toppled onto the floor, her attention only on the mirror and keeping her blood flowing over it. For Vardan. For his people.

But mostly for him.

The room began to dim, and she knew she'd lost too much blood to stay conscious for long. If she knew the curse was broken, perhaps she could heal herself, but that would mean seeing Vardan, and if his eyes met hers, her heart would break at his hatred when her heart held only love for him.

"Lady Belle!" The one voice she both desired and dreaded spoke her name, or at least the name he'd given her. "You're hurt. Let me help you. How did this happen?" He raised his voice to bellow, "Someone help! Lady Belle is hurt! Fetch a physician. A surgeon. Someone who can help!"

"Do not...worry. I did this. It is my fault, and I must...repair the damage." Drawing breath was becoming difficult, but still Zuleika tried to speak. "My name is not Belle."

"You are my Lady Belle, and I love you," Vardan said, his eyes softening as he smiled. Like a man, and not a beast. A good man. Not a monster.

Running footsteps skidded to a halt. "Lady Belle has returned, and she's hurt. Send a rider to town for a physician!" Inga hurried to Zuleika's side, lifting the skirt of her pink gown a little so it wouldn't slow her down. A gown Zuleika could see.

The curse was broken. She had not failed him. Now it didn't matter that her vision had grown dim.

"Lady Belle, what happened?" Vardan asked urgently.

"My name is Zuleika, and I have broken your curse. I never met you before this winter, and if I had, I never would have cast it." She closed her eyes. Oblivion hovered close now. She could feel it.

"But...why?" he whispered.

"Because I love you," she said.

He gathered her up in his arms, pressing her close, but she did not feel a thing, for she had already succumbed to the darkness' embrace.

Forty-One

Vardan jolted awake, convinced someone had doused him in Greek fire and set him alight, but his chamber was dark. Merely a dream, he told himself, but his dreams were reserved for Lady Belle, the maiden who always danced just out of reach.

His heart constricted in his chest at the thought of her. Too long had he resisted the siren call of the magic mirror. If he saw her but once, and knew she was safe, he would be content never to think of her again. Or if he were to discover her scheming with his brother…what then?

Then he would know that she was truly lost to him, and he could mourn.

Resolved, he climbed from his bed and padded to the library. In his childhood, the monks had worked there day and night, and true to tradition, the candles burned still. A warm wash of light to drive away the sudden chill in his heart.

Something was amiss. He could feel it.

Three steps into the room, he stopped dead.

She lay in a pool of blood, stretching out her hand for the magic mirror as if it could somehow help her.

He wanted to demand how she'd come here, where she'd gone, and who had hurt her, but most of all, he didn't want to lose her.

So much blood...

He bellowed for help as he dropped to his knees beside her, unsure what he could do. If he had a witch here now, he would trade his very soul for a spell that could save her life, but all he had were his two hands and a houseful of servants, none of whom knew magic or more than rudimentary healing.

He shouted for help again, and he saw her move, just the tiniest bit. Her face crumpled, as if in pain. She mumbled something that sounded like nonsense and he did his best to reassure her. Help would come. It had to.

A hand touched his shoulder. Fingers he could see.

Inga's voice roused the household, commanding them like an army in battle. Better she than him tonight. He couldn't turn his attention away from Belle. Couldn't lose her again.

She mumbled more nonsense before her eyes closed.

No. What cruel fate had returned her to him, only to kill her before his eyes?

"Why?" he begged of the heavens, but he got no answer except a sigh as Belle's breath left her.

Forty-Two

Zuleika opened her eyes, expecting an afterlife, but she only saw the dowager queen's bedchamber. She still lived. Her hand was terribly painful, and shrouded in linen bandages.

"The lady wakes." Vardan rose from his corner chair, much as he had the first time they met. Today, though, he was merely a man, and no longer a cursed creature. As Zuleika's gaze caressed his features for what she was certain would be the last time, she found it hard to believe she had ever mistaken him for his brother. Sure, both men had similar features, but the expression on Vardan's face and the soul shining through his eyes showed him to be a very different man. A man of honour, integrity, compassion and...for at least a little while, love.

"So many times I told you my tale, that I forgot to ask for yours. So, tell me, Lady Belle, or will you give me your true name now?"

She winced. "I already told you. The first name was a gift from you. It wasn't so different to my name. Not really. Zuleika means brilliant beauty. It is the name my parents gave me, and the rest of the world knows me by. Zuleika, enchantress, daughter of Baron Hans and his wife Lady Zoraida, also an enchantress, and the previous owner of the mirror enchanted with farseeing before I cursed it at the king's command." She swallowed painfully. "The very same mirror I smashed in your library."

Vardan drew the chair up beside the bed and seated himself. "It sounds like quite a tale, Lady Zuleika. Especially as I have heard that name before. I think I deserve to hear all of your tale now."

So Zuleika told him everything, starting with the king's courier, Sir Ryder, through to her escape from the palace. Tears rolled down her cheeks, but she didn't stop to wipe them away. She described trying to open a portal at the bottom of the sea, where her father's ship had sunk, and of finding herself in Vardan's courtyard. Finally, she told him about how she'd realised that the curse on Beacon Isle was indeed of her making, but magnified hundreds of times over, because of the mirror, and how she hadn't been sure she could break something so powerful, but she had owed it to him to try.

And when she was done, her vision so blurred by tears she could no longer see, Vardan walked out of the room without saying a word.

Her every instinct screamed to call him back, but she knew it would be no use. Vardan was free to live the life he deserved and love a woman as honourable as he was. Not a witch who was tainted with the darkness of her crimes.

Slowly, painfully, she pulled a gown over her shift, and made her way down to the courtyard. No one stopped her; no one even saw her. For a household that had once been full of invisible people, she was the only invisible one now without even a spell to make her so. No matter. She would not be here for long.

Zuleika bit her unbandaged finger and drew a doorway in the air. Her blood touched the earth and the circle was complete, opening a portal home. With one final glance back at the house on Beacon Isle, she stepped through the portal and left the island, and the prince, behind.

Forty-Three

By the time Lady Belle – no, Lady Zuleika – had finished her tale, Vardan wasn't sure whether he wanted to kill his brother outright or torture him for eternity. What Thorn had forced her to do, that she'd felt honour-bound to undo, even at the risk of her life...

He didn't want to believe it, but her eyes burned with sincerity through every word. How could he not believe her? The memory of her lying in all that blood was one he would never forget. Even now, she was deathly pale.

She had nearly given her life for him. If he'd taken the time to find out more about the curse earlier, he might have stopped using the mirror, might have saved her this pain. Damn him, if he'd taken his brother's advice and sought her out, even, none of this would have happened.

So when tears welled up in her eyes – tears because of the pain he'd caused her, through no fault of her own, he forced himself to leave the room. He had no right to embrace or comfort her, no matter how much he wanted to.

What comfort could he offer, anyway? She had run from him once. She didn't want him. But he was still deeply in her debt for breaking the curse.

She deserved vengeance for the wrongs Thorn had done her. Had done to them both.

Death wasn't good enough for him. And there was no honour in torture. Besides, Thorn expected some sort of attack from Vardan – he'd gone to great lengths to keep him here on the island, far from court. If Vardan did succeed in killing the king, he would be sentencing himself to a lifetime on the throne. A life he did not want, for his home was here. On a hill above what had once been the greatest trading port in the world. And would be again, he vowed.

If he couldn't take Thorn's life, he would take the one thing he loved most – his power. Thorn could keep his precious throne and his court. But Beacon Isle's storehouses contained the riches of most of the merchants in the civilised world. Merchants who knew Vardan to be their ally. If he could control the trade routes with the promise of keeping them free of pirates, his humble seat would hold more power than all the thrones in the western world combined.

But to do that, he needed Rolf.

He shouted for his steward as he strode to his solar, already listing names in his head. He knew which merchants held the most power among their colleagues, and he must win those over first. Had much changed in five years? Vardan needed to find out.

Rolf had a scruffy grey beard that made him look old. Vardan found himself staring at the man he hadn't seen for five years and wondering how the intervening time had aged him.

"You bellowed, master?" Rolf asked. "If you wanted to tell me the curse has been lifted, I noticed it for myself. You summoned me before I could shave."

"No. I've thought of a way to empty the cellars and the storehouses, and build a merchant league like the world has never seen before."

Rolf lifted an eyebrow. "White Harbour has hardly been open for a day and already you plan to fill it with ships?" His lips twitched with amusement.

Vardan hastened to explain his plan, as enthusiasm kindled in Rolf's eyes. Yes, he believed the idea was possible, and it was a good one. But he had so many questions and suggestions that Vardan had to reach for some paper to start writing it all down.

Vardan wasn't sure what time it was when Inga burst into the room. "Where is she?" the housekeeper demanded.

She'd grown thinner under the curse, he thought, though he couldn't be certain. "Where is who?" Vardan replied, before realisation froze his heart. Who else would drive her into such a panic but the Lady Zuleika?

"Lady Belle. She's not in her room," Inga said. "You were the last person to see her, master, and her so weak and all. She's supposed to stay in bed and rest. Where is she?"

In her panic, the woman looked like she was ready to shake him to make him talk. No one had dared try that on him since he was a boy.

"She was resting in bed when I saw her last. Search the house and the grounds, if you must. Send someone down to Harbourtown to enquire if anyone has seen her," Vardan said. "She's too ill to have gotten far."

Even as he said the words, he knew they were a lie. She could appear and vanish from his house at will, in a bolt of lightning. Weak as she was, had she run again? Not now. Surely not now.

"Find her," he said hoarsely. "Whatever it takes."

Inga marched out, so she didn't see Vardan grip the table to keep himself upright as his legs threatened to collapse beneath him.

"Are you well, master?" Rolf asked. He nodded at the prince's whitened knuckles.

Vardan passed a hand before his eyes. Without her, all his plotting would be a waste of time. She would be found, he told himself.

"I am well. Let us resume," Vardan said, and their discussion continued. Rolf recommended new names to add to the list of those to be approached first, then sent for inventories so they would know whose merchandise occupied the most space in the storehouses. Without the mirror and the invisible fleet, fighting pirates would be harder, but if they could persuade Zuleika to help with a spell or two…

Realisation hit Vardan like a blow. "The pirates. She turned them into scum."

"What did you say, master?"

"The pirates," Vardan repeated. "When the pirates attacked the *Trinity*, they disappeared, leaving nothing but green slime where they stood. She kept calling pirates scum, so that's what she turned them into. That's why I couldn't find a witch on the *Trinity*. She was here the whole time."

"So the Lady Belle truly was a witch?"

"Is a witch," Vardan corrected. "The Lady Zuleika,

for that is her real name, said she is an enchantress. A powerful sort of witch, I understand. One who has no need of ships or horses, for she can ride lightning."

"She sounds like a powerful ally to have. Is she on these lists yet?" Rolf asked.

Vardan swallowed. "She has helped us so much already. We are deeply in her debt. All this is a small way I can begin to repay her for what she has done."

"Most ladies like flowers, gowns and trinkets. Love letters and poetry, even," Rolf offered. "Jewels – I know she likes those. A league of merchants is hardly the way to woo a maiden."

"When the snow melts, I shall give her every rose in my garden, but until then...I would rather lay the world at her feet. The Lady Zuleika is not most ladies, my friend."

"No, that she's not," Rolf said softly. He clapped the prince on the back. "Now, until we can persuade a witch to turn your sailors invisible, I propose...."

They talked tactics for a long time, until the news arrived that she was nowhere to be found on the island. The lady had vanished as quickly as she'd arrived, just like before.

Feeling Rolf's eyes upon him, Vardan schooled the anguish away from his expression. "Then I shall stay here, while you act as my envoy to the merchants on my first list. Send word after every meeting, so that I might know the outcome. I want to know who is with us, and who is not, for the more who agree, the more the others will be swayed."

"And what of the lady?" Rolf asked.

Vardan's eyes flashed. "She is a merchant's daughter. Maybe even the daughter of one of the men on that list. She identified her father's mark on some of the goods in our cellar. If you see her on your travels...tell her....tell her..." He swallowed. "Tell her she is welcome at Beacon Isle at any time, for any reason, and that the contents of the library are hers, if she wants them."

Rolf whistled. "The monks won't like that."

"Bugger the monks. They left the books here with me when they deserted the island. They belong to the one person who saved it."

"Yes, master. When I find her, I'll tell her that." Rolf's eyes glinted.

When. Vardan liked that. When he found her. Until that time came, he would live in hope. For now he was a man again, hope was his once more.

Forty-Four

Weeks passed. The snow melted and the roads turned into a quagmire of mud. Then that, too, dried, until there was little to deter anyone but the most timid horseman from reaching her father's keep.

Zuleika expected the king's men hourly, knowing it was only a matter of time before he discovered that she'd lifted the curse at Beacon Isle and was once again within his borders. Within easy grasp. He might not have a powerful witch at his disposal, but she was still weak from losing so much blood. Casting more than the most minor spell would tax her strength, leaving her as helpless as any normal woman in the hands of a much stronger man, and she swore she would die before she let the king touch her again.

No man would, for her heart belonged to his brother.

So she waited, and rested, and while she rested, she read. She read every book and scroll in her mother's bower, and when she was finished, she read them again. Never again would she curse an object as she had her mother's mirror, at least not without some safeguard in place to prevent the curse from enchanting the same person more than once. And never without some loophole that would allow someone else to break the spell without spilling her blood.

It hadn't escaped her that if she'd created the very loophole the king had invented, her love for Vardan would have broken the spell weeks ago, and he would never have needed to know about her powers, or that she'd cast the curse in the first place. There was no point in wishing Thorn's lies were true, though. Even if she were to cast a spell on him so that any lie he told transformed into truth, it would be too late to help her.

So, sighing, she returned to her books. She'd heard whispers about a witch who could weave the fates of men into real cloth on her loom, and she wanted to know whether it was possible before she sought out the witch to stop her. Cursing men was one thing, but taking their free will and rewriting their destiny? That went too far. She wanted to believe that the woman was merely a seer whose skills allowed her to illuminate a man's path to his desired goal, but if the stories were correct, she demanded a high price from her would-be clients, and those who chose not to engage her services found themselves threatened with ruin in the most horrible ways.

Shouts from the courtyard below dragged her thoughts from the dry manuscript before her. More voices than there should be in her father's house right now. Her time had run out – the king's men had come for her.

Zuleika sighed. She might not be completely recovered, but she was well enough to cast a portal. Were they just in the main courtyard, or had they overrun the keep already? Zuleika peered out the window. If she could make it to the kitchen garden...

She gripped the window sill, forgetting about spells or escape. The courtyard was filled with laden wagons, and more were plodding up the road to the keep. The shouts she'd heard were orders for every able man in the household to help unload the goods Zuleika recognised from the storehouses on Beacon Isle. Vardan had kept his word, and returned everything.

Zuleika flew down the steps to her father's study, where she found him in deep discussion with a man whose voice she recognised as belonging to Rolf, Vardan's steward.

"I already told you, he will accept no payment for the return of your goods," Rolf said irritably. "He's done this as an act of goodwill, because he needs merchants like you to join with him in league against pirates and kings who make doing business impossible, and he knows the losses you have already suffered. He asks but one thing from you." Rolf's eyes darted in Zuleika's direction, though he did not meet her gaze. "That you send him the Lady Zuleika."

Father's face turned red. "That's preposterous. Sell my virgin daughter to a rebel who opposes the king? Better I send her to court, where she will find a husband whose armies will fight this insanity. Why, the king himself has expressed his interest in my daughter for a bride. I'll not have her sold into slavery to a man who holds me to ransom!"

"Prince Vardan does not buy or sell slaves, Father," Zuleika said. "If he seeks to set up a league of merchants, doubtless he has heard of how fast I can travel, and he wishes to engage my services as an envoy to turn this league into a reality before someone breathes word of it to the king. If you join him in this, as your daughter, the other merchants will listen to me. Wouldn't it be a relief to only have to lose your ship to a storm, instead of so many other things? If only to save your fortunes alone, I would go, but to set up lasting trade agreements across the world? It would be an honour, Father." Now she found Rolf staring at her, and she met his gaze without flinching. "If the prince wants me, he shall have me."

If only he wanted her the way she wanted him.

Forty-Five

Vardan surveyed White Harbour with satisfaction. The ships had returned, as he'd predicted, and many brought letters from the merchants who owned them. Pledges of support, paeans of praise for his ideas, requests for reductions in port duties when they docked at Beacon Isle...they came thick and fast, but still didn't have the power to bring a smile to his face. Only one person could do that – the Lady Zuleika, if she returned to him.

Or Rolf, if he sent a letter saying the lady was on her way.

He ripped open the last letter and skimmed the first lines. This one was far from complimentary. The merchant who'd sent it couldn't decide whether Vardan was insane or merely a traitor, but he swore the king would hear of it, all the same. Vardan peered at the seal, trying to remember the man. Ah, now he knew him. He was the younger brother to the crone Thorn had tried to marry him to, years ago. That made him the king's man, or a man the king wanted to court.

Vardan was tempted to throw the letter into the fire and be done with it, but caution stayed his hand. Yes, Thorn would certainly hear of their merchant league, but there was little he could do about it when he did. That was the beauty of it – many ports were already in the hands of those who had been first to support Vardan. Even if Thorn sent troops or ships to attack Beacon Isle, they were one port among dozens around the world, in countries Thorn did not control. And the one port which had a fleet experienced in naval warfare and combating pirates.

Once Thorn realised his impotence, he would lash out at anyone who got in his way – especially those who brought bad tidings. Loyalty to King Thorn did not always mean a reward, for Vardan knew how treacherous his brother could be.

Vardan found paper and ink, and began to write a response to the merchant who called him mad. The man might be old and loyal, but he was not entirely stupid, and if he liked living, perhaps he would be willing to embrace what he'd once called madness. If he did not...be it on his own head. He could stand with the treacherous snake. Vardan had more men than he needed on his side already.

But all the men in the world could not equal one woman...

He sighed and sent up a silent prayer that someone would find her, and persuade Zuleika to return to him. If word of the league reached Thorn, it would surely reach her.

He hoped so. For all this was for naught unless one day he would be reunited with his Lady Belle.

Forty-Six

Some hours later, when the only thing in the wagons was a chest of Zuleika's belongings that looked pitiful compared to the full loads they'd carried up to the keep, Rolf offered her a seat beside her chest, but Zuleika declined. She was far more comfortable astride her own horse, even if little Lady was nowhere near as elegant as the prince's Embarr.

She rode tall and straight, like the queen her father had wanted her to be. He'd settle for her being a princess, though, she'd discovered, when she'd found him interrogating Rolf about the prince, particularly whether he had a wife. Her father had insisted she wear her violet riding habit, and do everything she could to make the prince think of her as a suitable bride, not an envoy.

Privately, she wasn't even sure he'd consider her an envoy, but the more she thought about the idea, the more she liked it. She would never be a bride, let alone Vardan's, but his merchant league had merit. Not to mention it would give him allies against the king, should Thorn choose a less devious attack than a curse. And she would get to see him again.

Rolf coughed, making her look up. He looked relieved to have finally secured her attention. "Beg pardon, my lady. But is it true what the master said about you being a witch?"

She considered not telling him, but where was the harm in telling the man what he already knew? Vardan kept no secrets from his servants, after all.

Zuleika sighed. "Yes. And when I was a child, I cursed a mirror on the king's command, which he gave to the prince. When I arrived at your island and discovered the result of the cursed gift, I did everything in my power to undo the harm that was done. I could not give back the lost time, or make up for all those years of invisibility, or – "

"Is it true that you nearly died to break the curse?" Rolf interrupted.

"Yes," she admitted, then hastened to add, "But I am much recovered from the ordeal. Why, I'm sure I could cast a spell before you could blink, if I needed to." Not that he looked about to attack her for being a witch, but it paid to be wary.

"Like the fast travel spell you talked about. Is that how you appeared on the island?"

Zuleika nodded. "I could, but I'm not sure I'd have the power to create a portal big enough to fit all of us, including the wagons. In fact, my portals are barely large enough for me. Certainly not big enough for a horse."

Rolf wet his lips. "So, if you wanted to, you could go back to Beacon Isle without having to take ship with us, and be there sooner. Like, today?"

And see Vardan sooner. "Yes."

"Then you should go, my lady. The master was very angry when you disappeared just as the curse broke. He said if we found you, to send you to him immediately."

Zuleika's traitorous heart beat faster at the faint hope that Vardan wanted to see her again. Perhaps he had questions about her past. Or he wanted to tell her to her face that she was no longer welcome on Beacon Isle, as if walking out of the room when she'd finished her tale wasn't clear enough.

"You would not mind?" she asked.

Rolf grinned. "I've been cursed for five years, my lady, but I never saw magic cast before. Seems you're the good kind of witch, lifting the curse and all, so if I see any magic, I'd like it to be yours."

"A witch like me is called an enchantress. There are not many of us, and fewer still can cast portals," Zuleika said. "We try to do some good in the world."

"As you will, my lady." Rolf reined in his horse, and waited.

Zuleika slid from Lady's back, feeling very self-conscious with Rolf watching. Portal magic was difficult, but not particularly impressive. She bit her finger, and traced an arch in the air, squeezing out a drop of blood to hit the earth at the end. The portal to Beacon Isle glowed into life.

"Farewell, my lady. We will see you at Beacon Isle soon," she heard Rolf say as she stepped through.

Forty-Seven

As Vardan strode along the passage, he glimpsed a flash of purple in the rose garden. Could it be she? Instead of leaning out the window, he raced down the stairs into the courtyard. Row upon row of rosebushes stood sentinel…but no lady lay among them.

It was probably a good thing. While snow had lain deep in the courtyard when she first arrived, now she would find herself beset by thorns.

He approached the place where he'd first seen her. In place of the snowdrift, there stood a different white drift – this time made up of rose petals, not snow, as his grandmother's white roses were celebrating spring in true floral form. She'd called them her full moon roses, specially bred for their colour, which in the ancient language of flowers meant loyalty.

Here he saw the purple he'd glimpsed from the level above. In the midst of all the white roses, one rosebush had not yet burst into bloom as its companions had. No, this had extended a stem higher than any of the others, and it was crowned by a single bud that had just begun to open.

This rose was not white, like its fellows, but a particular shade of purple. Almost exactly like the pair of enchanting eyes that haunted his dreams.

For that was the meaning of purple roses, he remembered now: enchantment.

His grandmother would have liked the blue moon among all her full moons. She probably would have liked Zuleika, too – the lady who undoubtedly changed the colour of her roses through magical means.

Smiling, Vardan stretched out on one of the garden benches his grandmother had liked to sit on when he was a boy.

Throughout the rest of the house and Harbourtown below, people bustled about their business, but he enjoyed a moment of stillness. His grandmother's garden always brought him peace.

Forty Eight

Spring had come to Vardan's rose garden far sooner than it had reached her father's house, Zuleika found. Some of the bushes had already burst into bloom, while the profusion of buds on others promised that spring had only just begun.

It was a far cry from the snow-filled courtyard she'd first arrived in. And so sweet-smelling, too. Zuleika took another deep breath, hoping that the memory of sweetness would be enough to help her keep her composure in her interview with Vardan. No, she would need more than just the memory. Reaching out, she plucked a purple rose from the nearest bush, and tucked the bloom into her braided hair.

"Now you've returned to steal my flowers, Lady Belle?"

Zuleika whirled and found Vardan seated on a bench she hadn't seen, tucked under an archway twined with flowers. He rose.

"I...I didn't mean to..." she stammered. "And my name isn't – "

"Belle, I know," he interrupted. "But you have been Lady Belle to me so long, both before me and in my dreams, it is hard to remember you are also Lady Zuleika, powerful enchantress." He bowed.

Zuleika swallowed. "My power is less than it was," she admitted. "I lost a lot of blood. It will return, though, as I recover. Which reminds me that I have a proposal for you. When I heard of your plan for a merchants' league – "

"You came here with a proposal because of the merchants' league?" Disbelief registered on his face.

Zuleika shook her head. "No, I came because Rolf brought my father's goods, and told him that they came at a price. That I must come here immediately."

"I gave no such order," he snapped, then his voice softened as he continued, "Though I considered it. Many times. Rolf..."

Realisation hit Zuleika at the same time as she saw it dawn in Vardan's eyes. "He lied," she breathed. "Loyalty. He lied to me out of loyalty to you, so that I would return to Beacon Isle. To you." His eyes. Once she'd seen them, she couldn't look away. Beast or man, those eyes spoke to her soul as he pierced her heart. She understood the loyalty that had driven Rolf. Now, she, too, would live or die for this man. Even if he never looked at her the same way as he had the night he'd kissed her.

She cleared her throat. "To be your envoy, I assume, as I suggested. I can travel quickly, and if I speak for both you and my father, I'm sure your league will exist before the year is out. If you give me a list of merchants, I shall go immediately – "

"You will not. Rolf and my men have the league well in hand." Vardan took a deep breath. "If you wish to help me, I have a different proposal in mind. One where you stay here on Beacon Isle, with me. If you wish."

"Of course, but I thought…after I was the cause of the curse afflicting your island, you wouldn't want me here. No one would."

Vardan grasped her hand. "You cursed a mirror, not me. My brother gave me a cursed mirror, not you. I looked into the mirror and cursed my island, not you. Yet you came to my aid, to our aid, and broke the curse, though it nearly killed you. None of this is your fault, Lady Zuleika."

She swallowed. "But it is. I still cast the curse so the

211

king could give it to you. I had no idea it would be so powerful. Lifting it was the least I could do, when I knew no one else would be willing to die in order to correct my mistake. What else could I do?"

"I can think of a few things." He captured her other hand and brought them to his lips. A warm, tingling kiss drove all other thoughts out of her head for one blissful moment. "You are the only person alive who could break that curse?"

"Yes."

"And yet my brother told me to slay you."

Zuleika frowned. "That would not have broken the curse. The mirror was imbued with blood magic that only blood could dispel. Killing me would have ensured the curse was permanent."

Vardan inclined his head. "As you say. A curse my brother made you cast, which he gifted to me, and then lied about how to break it. He has woven a curious web to trap us both and keep us apart. Perhaps he fears what we can do together."

"With the league, yes – " she began, but he silenced her with a kiss. A kiss that stole her breath and her senses, because she wanted nothing more than him.

"With you by my side, he wouldn't dare try to curse me again," Vardan said. "Lady Zuleika, my brave Belle, would you do me the honour of becoming my wife?"

Zuleika felt lightheaded. For a moment, she

thought she'd heard him say something else, something impossible, until she realised she must have heard wrong. Her soaring heart plummeted. "Your witch?" she asked. "I could cast protection spells on your person right away, but to protect the isle would take longer. I would be honoured to try, though."

He chuckled. "I have had enough of spells to last me a lifetime, and perhaps a second one after that. No, I want you to be my wife. The woman who will stand by my side when the league first meets."

Zuleika's heart soared once more. There could be no mistake this time. "I will," she said, lifting her chin.

"You will? You really will?" He beamed. "I will send someone to bring a priest directly. We will be married in the chapel today, and tonight..." He swallowed, his eyes shining. "Tonight I will truly make you my wife. Nothing would make me happier."

Could he truly mean that? With all her heart, Zuleika wanted to believe him.

Forty-Nine

She'd agreed to stay. With him. His Lady Belle would be his in truth – tonight!

Vardan could barely believe it. That very morning, he'd wondered if he'd ever see her again. Now…he could scarcely stand to let her out of his sight. Inga refused to allow him into the queen's chambers, though, saying that it was bad luck to see a bride before she was ready for the wedding.

Vardan had endured enough bad luck for a lifetime – as had she. Reluctantly, he retreated from his housekeeper's stern gaze. He'd do nothing else to jeopardise his future with Zuleika. She'd run from him twice now, and he didn't want to risk a third time. Not when she was so close to becoming his wife.

And tonight…

Vardan swallowed. He'd endured so long without a woman's touch, that the mere thought of bedding Lady Belle tonight…he prayed that he could be the charming prince she deserved, and not a beast in her bed tonight.

Fifty

In a daze, Zuleika found herself back in her old chamber, at the mercy of a delighted Inga and Greta. Some time later, she stood in the chapel wearing the same gold silk dress she'd worn when she danced with the prince. When she knelt, he dropped to his knees at her side, and they both said the vows which the priest told them made them husband and wife.

The moment they left the chapel, Vardan pulled her in close to give her another breath-stealing kiss. Zuleika thought he would carry her to bed then and there, for the desire in his eyes was unmistakeable, but he insisted on heading for the great hall instead for supper.

She ate, but she didn't taste a bite. As each moment ticked past, it brought her closer to what she feared most about marriage. Even to Vardan. And yet…she did not want to delay the inevitable. When Vardan asked whether she wanted to dance a little after dinner, she summoned her courage and replied calmly, "No, I think I would like to go to bed."

Servants whispered as Vardan wrapped a proprietary arm around her waist and lifted her from her seat, but Zuleika did her best to ignore them. Her heart beat so fast she was scared he would hear it, but Vardan only took her hand and led her to a part of the house she hadn't seen before.

His bedchamber, she realised, entering the grand room that was much bigger than her windowless chamber. The bed, too, was enormous – big enough for a dozen people to sleep in. Fit for a king, or, tonight, a prince. And his bride.

Tears sprang to her eyes, though she tried to stop them. Vardan had his back to her now as he poured two cups of wine, but in a moment he would turn and see…

"You are the bravest woman I have ever met. One who, I believed until this day, was afraid of nothing. Yet now, you look terrified." He handed her a brimming cup. "Share the wine with me, and tell me your secret: what has the power to frighten an enchantress?"

She burst into tears. "The consummation."

"Ah." He sipped from his cup. "Me, too."

She stared at him. "Why?"

"The first time I kissed you, you ran away. If you found one kiss so terrible, what will you do if I don't please you in bed?"

Zuleika blushed. "It was not the kiss I objected to, but...has anyone ever told you how similar you look to your brother?" Her eyes begged him to understand.

Vardan clenched his fists. "One day, I will make sure my brother answers for the evil he has done. Whether to me, or to God, I haven't decided, but I swear on your life and mine, he will answer for it. I am not my brother, and I promise you that I will never hurt you. Never."

Zuleika wiped her tears away. "Not intentionally, no, but..." She felt like such a fool.

He seemed to understand. He sat on the edge of the bed, patting the spot beside him. When she sat, he said, "You drink your wine, for it's my turn to tell you a secret I never told anyone."

She sipped, and tasted dewberry wine. Relaxing a little, she said, "All right."

Vardan slipped an arm around her waist. "When I was perhaps sixteen or seventeen, only a boy though I thought I was a man, I was sent here to the monastery to study. My brother had just claimed the throne and perhaps he thought it amusing to make a monk of me. My grandmother had other ideas. One memorable week, an envoy came into port, from some exotic southern city. My grandmother wanted to hold a feast, so I was invited to sup with them. The envoy was boring, droning about politics and trade agreements that held no interest for me, but he'd brought with him two girls I thought were his daughters. As a good host, I set about trying to entertain them with witty conversation."

Zuleika managed a small smile. "Were you as charming then as you are now? I'm sure they could not resist you."

Vardan coughed. "I was a bumbling fool, and they knew it. As the evening progressed, though, it turned out that the ladies were not his daughters, but courtesans who he'd brought to soften up the monarchs he met along the way. As I was a prince, they decided that included me, so they made a wager as to who could win my affections by the end of the evening. After a few cups of wine, they called off the wager, and retired to their chamber with me in tow.

"They made a man of me that night, but as I was young and eager and had little stamina, the ladies took to amusing themselves. I watched, wide-eyed, for some time, before I summoned the courage to ask them what they were doing. So…they showed me everything they knew about how to pleasure a woman, and in the morning, one of them bit her lip the same way you do and whispered to me that when I lay with the woman I loved, I would give her nothing but pleasure, every time. I don't know if she was a witch, but the way she spoke and the way she touched me, it seemed very much like a spell."

Zuleika wet her lips. "Only an enchantress could work that sort of spell, and I haven't seen any magic about you since the curse was lifted."

Vardan reddened. "Well, no, you wouldn't. She only touched me in one place, which you haven't yet seen."

Zuleika took a deep breath. "Show me." She gulped a mouthful of wine.

He laughed nervously. "As my lady commands." He shucked off his clothes until he stood naked before her. "There. My…manhood."

As it was level with her eyes, it was hard not to stare. She'd known Vardan wasn't a small man, and this part of him wasn't small, either. She concentrated hard, and found she could see the glow of what might be a spell, though certainly not one of hers. This glowed faintly blue, instead of her familiar shades of purple. She reached out and wrapped her fingers around him, feeling the pulse of his heartbeat but also the throb of what was definitely a spell.

He groaned. "If you're going to do that, I won't last long enough to consummate this marriage. Can you do something more useful with your hands, like help me unlace your gown?"

She drained her wine cup, set it on the table, and found herself in Vardan's embrace. His lips tasted of dewberry as he kissed her deeply. Between them, they managed to remove Zuleika's gown and the shift beneath it, until she stood in nothing but her silk stockings.

Vardan held her at arm's length for a moment, drinking her in. "You are the most beautiful woman I've ever seen. I hope I don't disappoint you."

He kissed her again, pulling her close. As their bare bodies touched, it felt like the lightning spell had ignited along her skin, but it hurt neither of them. They toppled sideways onto the bed, her hands caressing the hard muscles of a man for the first time in her life and she found she quite liked it. Harder still was his manhood pressed against her leg. She wrapped her hand around it again…

"Oh God, you don't know how much I want to be inside you. I love you, Lady Belle," he groaned.

…and guided him between her thighs. She gasped as he filled her, expecting to feel pain, but instead there was just the wondrous warmth of his body joined with hers, inside hers, as she urged him to show her what he meant by pleasure.

He found a perfect rhythm, surging in and out of her with as much gentleness as if it truly was her first time, as his kisses grew more heated and his hands...oh, his hands. Stroking every inch of her until she wanted to purr like a cat. But there was a different sound fighting to escape from her throat, as a sort of storm welled up inside her. Stronger than the tide, sweeping her away, she heard her own cry of joy mingling with his.

When she regained her breath, she asked, "What was that?"

Vardan chuckled. "That is what happens when a chivalrous man makes love to a woman. The lady must always come first." When he withdrew from her, she noticed that the glow around his manhood was gone, but she didn't mention it, for her glow of happiness was more than enough for both of them, she was certain.

Later that night, after they'd made love for the third blissful time, Zuleika privately decided that the courtesan's pleasure spell hadn't done much, because Vardan was such an incredible lover already. So she cuddled up to her princely husband, who was no longer a beast except in bed, which suited her just fine, and dreamily resolved that they would live happily ever after.

Author's Note

If you're looking for more fairy tale retellings…here's a sneak peek from *Awaken: Sleeping Beauty Retold*, the next book in the series.

Bonus Sneak Peek

Awaken: Sleeping Beauty Retold

"You should be here, planning a coronation ceremony and ruling the kingdom. Not riding about, chasing birds in the woods!" Lady Schutz hissed.

Lord Siward sighed. "Grandmother, this kingdom is so small, it almost rules itself. And it has been scarcely three weeks since the king died. The earth has not even had time to settle over his grave. It would be an insult to his memory to attempt to steal his throne before we know whether an heir can be found."

"Normal kingdoms name a new king on the same day the old one dies. A kingdom should not be without a ruler for even a day!" she insisted.

"If only our kingdom could be normal, but it is not. Neither is it without a ruler. I am not leaving the kingdom. I am simply riding out of the city for a little while. I shall visit the borders and the outlying villages, make sure all is well, and if I choose to spend a day or two hawking, what of it? It is the sport of kings, after all, and you are so set on me becoming one. It seems to me I should enjoy some of the privileges, seeing as I already shoulder the burdens of a position which are not mine to bear."

She threw her wrinkled hands up into the air. "Be it on your own head, then, if some other noble tries to claim the throne while you are playing with birds!"

"If some madman attempts it, then he is welcome to the throne," Lord Siward snapped. If only another man would lay claim to that much-vaunted chair, then he could do the job his father had done, instead of trying to rule in the king's stead. If they could find an heir...

But there was no heir. The king and queen had managed to have one child, and she had died young. A normal kingdom could ask for a near relation who had married into one of the royal families of a neighbouring kingdom, but this was no normal kingdom.

So that left him. Siward sighed, knowing he would

have to ascend the throne on his return. No other man in court was capable of ruling, though others had blood far more noble than his. Yet the king on his deathbed had appointed him regent, for his sins.

All the more reason to take this trip now, for it might be his last chance at freedom before the heavy yoke of kingship settled on his shoulders.

His head started to clear as he left the city. Perhaps it was the lack of courtly arse-kissing, or maybe it was the clean scent from the woods instead of the smoke from cookfires, but he took heart when the city walls vanished from sight.

It was easily a week's ride to the border by way of the main road, but checking the borders was his first task. Every year, like his father and grandfather before him, Siward rode the borders, checking for signs of weakness. He hadn't found one yet, but if ever there was a time he needed one...it was now.

When he arrived at the end of the road, Siward sighed. He hadn't expected any change, though he had hoped for one.

Bramble hedges soared into the sky, forming a wall more formidable than simple stone. This wall ringed the kingdom, allowing no one in or out, and it had stood since his grandfather's time. His grandfather, Lord Schutz, had said the Wall had been a simple hedge once, but when the princess passed, the plants had risen up in protest to protect the kingdom. Siward never understood what they protected the kingdom from, for his grandfather had rambled considerably in his old age. Sometimes, he'd said it was to prevent a plague. At other times, he'd insisted it was to prevent war with a neighbouring kingdom, who had apparently killed the princess.

The truth of the tale was lost in time – and with his grandfather, who had lain in his grave for many years now.

Yet the Wall still stood, testament to some mysterious truth. Perhaps someone had cursed the kingdom, Siward decided. It seemed as good an explanation as any. But if it weren't for the Wall, he could send messengers to neighbouring kingdoms to search for an heir. With it...he would be king.

The first time he'd seen the Wall, Siward had slashed at it with his sword, determined like a hundred other men before him that he could cut his way through. The brambles would have none of it, wrapping tendrils around his sword until they dragged it from his hand as they repaired the damage to the Wall as though he had never sliced a single stroke. The Wall was magic, most certainly. Which made it all the harder for a soldier like himself to understand. There were no witches in the kingdom, so whoever had cast it must be on the other side of the Wall, and out of his reach.

Astor, his hunting hawk, ruffled her feathers as if impatient to do something more than sit on her perch.

"You have the right of it, my friend," Siward told the bird, pulling off the creature's hood. "Let us hunt, and forget politics for a time. Worrying about it will not bring down the Wall."

He headed off the road, toward a spot known only to his family. It had the best hawking in the kingdom, and so it would continue as long as its location remained a closely-kept secret. Not even his grandmother knew this spot, he'd wager, for she had no desire to hunt.

He unhooded Astor, held his fist high in the air, and watched the bird fly off with powerful wingbeats. Siward wished for a moment that he could fly with her, high above the Wall, to see the world outside. Was it so different to their kingdom? As long as the Wall stood, he would never know.

With his eyes on Astor, Siward urged his horse to follow the bird. The forest was not so dense here, though there was no village nearby. Perhaps there once had been one, but it had been too close to the border that before the Wall it had been attacked too many times until it had been abandoned. Surely there would have been some ruins left, then, to mark where the town had stood. Yet Siward had never seen them.

Perhaps the brambles and briars had consumed those, too.

Astor hovered, and Siward held his breath for a moment before the hawk dived, gracefully seizing a bird on the wing before her prey had even been aware of her presence. Astor swooped down with her catch still in her talons, toward a briar-shrouded rock.

Siward thought she would perch on the rock, but Astor dipped down behind it and disappeared. Swearing, he rode around, trying to find the bird, but the rock seemed solid on all sides, and the bird was nowhere in sight. He called her and heard an answering cry, but she did not reappear.

He swore again. The rock must be hollow, and his bloody bird was in the middle of it. If he didn't catch her before she devoured her prey, he'd lose her as a hunting hawk. Bird be damned, but she was his best, and he was loath to lose her. If there was no other way in, he would have to climb.

Siward had not climbed rocks or trees since he was a boy, but he was not so old that he did not enjoy doing it again. Just as long as his grandmother or his future subjects didn't catch him behaving like a youth.

The rock had a surprising number of easy toeholds for him, so it wasn't long until Siward had reached the top. The view he saw from his vantage point, though, made his mouth fall open in surprise. What he had taken for a rock was in fact a sprawling building – he'd been climbing the walls. Astor, bright bird that she was, had perched on a wall that had partially fallen down, hiding her from his sight until now. He called her again, but the stubborn bird did not move.

Siward swore again. He would have to fetch her. At least it would be a simple matter of walking along the walls to her current spot, scooping her up and hooding her once more.

He could not keep his eyes on the bird and his footing, though, and by the time he looked up, the blasted bird had moved to a wall in the middle of the building. She teetered there for a moment, before diving into the room below.

Siward made his way to the spot where he'd last seen Astor, and stopped. Below him was a courtyard, free of the collapsed roof fragments most of the other rooms had sported. Yet it was not the courtyard that drew his eye, but the incredibly lifelike statue of a woman in the middle of it, surrounded by roses.

Made of alabaster or white marble, she looked as though she would open her eyes and rise at any moment. Some virgin goddess or the Queen of Heaven, Siward guessed, depending on how old the statue was. Yet it looked newly carved, not as though it had been lying in this ruin for centuries, as surely it had been. A wondrous work of art indeed.

If he had to take the throne, he would place this statue in the throne room, so that every time he was bored, he could stare at her and wonder what her story was, and remember how he'd found her on his last days of freedom.

Siward jumped down from the wall, bending his knees to cushion the impact of his landing. Good thing, too, for the ground beneath his feet was harder than he expected. Swiping his booted foot through the leaf litter, he pushed aside the thin layer to reveal a mosaic floor of remarkable craftsmanship, though it paled into insignificance when compared to the magnificent statue.

Now he was closer, she looked even more divine. Like his every desire made flesh – or stone, at least. Siward laughed at himself. A statue so real it stirred his loins. Perhaps becoming king would not be such a bad thing. He would be expected to take a queen, and ensure a clear succession. That would stop him from lusting after statues.

No, he decided, inspecting the goddess, for no real woman could look so perfect. He must have this statue in his throne room.

He reached out to touch the stone, to see what fastened her to the plinth below. Perhaps he could move her out of here and send someone to collect the statue, so that it would be in place when he returned.

If she had been fastened by her feet and fallen over at some point, he might be able to…

A briar shot out, twining around his wrist so fast he could not move it. "What in blazes – " he began, only now realising that the plants had sent tendrils around both of his legs and his other arm, too. A thicker branch snaked around his middle, yanking him away from the statue.

Siward shouted for help, but he was alone in the ruin, as he well knew.

No, not quite alone.

Astor, his traitorous bird, landed on the plinth beside the statue's shoulder and peered at the goddess' face, as though working out what her lips would taste like. That beak could chip stone, and ruin the statue. The bird had caused enough trouble today.

"No!" Siward commanded. "Leave the girl alone. She is not to be harmed."

Finally deciding to be obedient, the bird flew off, perching on the wall once more.

Siward breathed a sigh of relief. She was safe.

He thought he heard something rustling through the leaves, and turned his attention back to the statue. What he saw stole his breath and his voice.

For the statue's closed eyes now stood open, green as emeralds, as she stared back at him.

The tale continues in the next book in the series
Awaken:
Sleeping Beauty Retold

About the Author

Demelza Carlton has always loved the ocean, but on her first snorkelling trip she found she was afraid of fish.

She has since swum with sea lions, sharks and sea cucumbers and stood on spray drenched cliffs over a seething sea as a seven-metre cyclonic swell surged in, shattering a shipwreck below.

Demelza now lives in Perth, Western Australia, the shark attack capital of the world.

The *Ocean's Gift* series was her first foray into fiction, followed by her suspense thriller *Nightmares* trilogy. She swears the *Mel Goes to Hell* series ambushed her on a crowded train and wouldn't leave her alone.

Want to know more? You can follow Demelza on Facebook, Twitter, YouTube or her website, Demelza Carlton's Place at:

www.demelzacarlton.com

Books by Demelza Carlton

Ocean's Gift series

Ocean's Gift (#1)

Ocean's Infiltrator (#2)

Ocean's Depths (#3)

Water and Fire

Turbulence and Triumph series

Ocean's Justice (#1)

Ocean's Trial (#2)

Ocean's Triumph (#3)

Ocean's Ride (#4)

Ocean's Cage (#5)

Ocean's Birth (#6)

How To Catch Crabs

Nightmares Trilogy

Nightmares of Caitlin Lockyer (#1)

Necessary Evil of Nathan Miller (#2)

Afterlife of Alana Miller (#3)

Mel Goes to Hell series

Welcome to Hell (#1)
See You in Hell (#2)
Mel Goes to Hell (#3)
To Hell and Back (#4)
The Holiday From Hell (#5)
All Hell Breaks Loose (#6)

Romance Island Resort series

Maid for the Rock Star (#1)
The Rock Star's Email Order Bride (#2)
The Rock Star's Virginity (#3)
The Rock Star and the Billionaire (#4)
The Rock Star Wants A Wife (#5)
The Rock Star's Wedding (#6)
Maid for the South Pole (#7)
Jailbird Bride (#8)

The Complex series

Halcyon

Romance a Medieval Fairytale series

Enchant: Beauty and the Beast Retold (#1)
Awaken: Sleeping Beauty Retold (#2)
Dance: Cinderella Retold (#3)